Always YOURS

HEARTS OF DANGER

SHIRLEY SIATON

ALWAYS YOURS
Hearts of Danger

Copyright © 2023 Shirley Siaton-Parabia

ALL RIGHTS RESERVED.

No part of this book may be reproduced or used in any manner without the prior written permission of the copyright owner, except for the use of brief quotations in a book review. To request permission, contact the publisher at books@inkysword.com.

This is a work of fiction. Names, characters, businesses, events and incidents are the products of the author's imagination. Any resemblance to actual persons, living or dead, or actual events is purely coincidental.

All brand and product names used in this book are trademarks, registered trademarks, or trade names of their respective owners. Inky Sword Book Publishing is not associated with any product or vendor in this book.

ISBN 978-6-21-060816-8 (pbk)
ISBN 978-6-21-490001-5 (Kindle

First Edition, March 2023

Published by Shirley S. Parabia

Inky Sword Book Publishing
Barangay Quezon, Arevalo, Iloilo City 5000
Republic of the Philippines
inkysword.com

Content Warnings

Warnings for explicit content, mild profanity, and references to violence and murder.

Recommended for mature readers 18 years old and above.

To Peter, our capo di tutti capi
Yours, always

Table of Contents

Book III: Shadow and Light

Acknowledgments

I am very grateful to *Glitter Magazine Philippines*, *MOD Filipina Magazine*, and *The Accounts* (University of the Philippines-Visayas) for publishing my works 'Hobo,' 'Storms,' and 'Dancing in the Rain,' respectively, the inspiration for the novellas in the collection.

My gratitude to Eve of Harbinger Design for the gorgeous book cover and to Mhy San Miguel for formatting this manuscript beautifully.

Finally, many thanks and lots of love to my mother, Mimi, for encouraging me to bring my short stories back to life.

Always
YOURS
HEARTS OF DANGER

BOOK I
Angel

Playlist

"My Heart"
Paramore

"Secret Love Song"
Little Mix & Jason Derulo

"Dusk till Dawn"
Zayn & Sia

"Going Under"
Evanescence

"Hero"
Enrique Iglesias

"Put Your Arms Around Me"
Texas

ONE

Stranger

She gazed at the sky for probably the umpteenth time in the past hour.

It was a starry night. The North Star and the many known constellations stood out clearly, brightly. The moon was bright and perfectly spherical. There was no chance of rain.

It was the kind of night for romance, at least for a teenaged girl.

Stella Montero sat by herself at the street corner. The bench, with a newly dried coat of fresh paint, courtesy of a congressman, was right by the bus stop.

This was her favorite intersection, one she had grown up in. It was always brightly-lit by traffic lights and neon storefront signs. Green, red, orange, yellow and blue; it was its own kind of rainbow.

A gust of wind blew, stirring the street before her. Discarded newspapers and fliers flew by, tumbling on the stone pavement decorated by graffiti as colorful as the lights overhead.

Stella looked at the sky again. In mere seconds, it seemed to have grown murky and cloudy, as if someone had stolen the lights.

The stars were not the only ones that disappeared that night. Her hopes had gone, too.

Was it only this afternoon when Aaron called and asked if she wanted to go to the movies with him? Was it only a few hours ago when she, drifting on fluffy white clouds, had put on her best dress and favorite shoes and snuck into her mother's room to use her makeup and perfume?

She had already fallen from those clouds. More like stumbled, fell, and landed on the cold hard ground on her ass.

Six-thirty, the time she was supposed to meet Aaron Soler, had come and gone.

It was getting cold. She looked at her watch. It was already half past eight. She pulled her now-rumpled white cardigan more tightly around her body, shoving her hands into their shallow pockets. She would be an idiot if she allowed herself any more hope that he would show up at all. She had more self-respect than that.

"Stood you up, hasn't he?" The voice came out of nowhere, causing her to nearly jump out of her skin.

She sprang to her feet and backed a few feet away, hands clenching into fists as she turned to face the owner of the voice.

She had a box cutter in her bag, she thought, comforted. A girl who grew up in a city like hers knew how to protect herself.

He emerged from underneath the awning of an ice cream shop.

It was a boy. No, a man, tall and dangerous-looking as any predator of the shadows.

He had a thick mane of hair that fell past his shoulders. His skin was duskier than most, allowing him to blend easier into the night. Most of his face was still shrouded in the darkness; what she could see was about a third of his profile, sharp and harsh.

He was the most fearsome and compelling sight she had ever laid eyes on.

"Who are you?" It was almost a shriek, nothing like her own voice. "What do you want?"

He advanced into the light. His face looked even harder and older. There was a scar that ran the length of his right cheek, hidden in part by his long hair. He appeared to be in his early twenties, perhaps older.

"My name is Trey," he said, almost formally. "Hello, Stella."

She backed further away, hot and cold rushing through her veins at the same time.

"How did you know my name?" she demanded.

He gave a slight shrug, his shoulders rippling. "I asked."

She drew herself to her full height of five-foot-five, enough to intimidate most boys her age. It would probably have no effect on him, seeing that he was much bigger, but there was no harm in trying to appear braver than she actually was. "Asked who?"

"The people here. Everyone knows you."

"The people?" she echoed, stumped.

"You see them every day."

She stared, trying to understand what he meant.

Them? The people?

She blinked, slightly taken aback by the bright light coming out of the open doorway of the leather repair shop down the street. She shut her eyes for the briefest of moments. When she opened them, she saw the sweet old woman who ran the shop give her a smile and a friendly wave. Seconds later, someone else left the shop, the old man who did all the repairs by hand or using an ancient pedal machine.

She watched them lock up the shop and walk off.

She understood.

This was her intersection, her neighborhood, her city.

"Yes," she said, more to herself than to the stranger. "I see them every day."

"So you do."

She glared up at him, feeling infinitely more confident that she did minutes ago. "That doesn't explain why you're here, or what you want from me."

"With you? Nothing." Trey sat on the bench she had vacated, draping his arm over the back of the seat and extending his legs. With his dark shirt and jeans, he looked like a giant snake, coiled and poised to strike. "Why I'm here has everything to do with your friend, the pretty boy."

"Aaron?"

"We were tipped off by one of his sidekicks. They come here and pick up girls for their pot sessions. The last one didn't go so well. Joshua didn't want to be part of the repeat performance."

'Pretty boy' Aaron, who was supposed to be her date, was a senior and the most popular boy at their college. His father was the mayor of one of the smaller towns that bordered the city. Aaron always had a lot of boys in his entourage, mostly those from more affluent families; they moved around the school as if they owned it. Girls who got his attention instantly became the most popular ones at school. With her being only a freshman, his initial attentions had flattered Stella to no end.

"Joshua." She repeated the name, trying to jog her memory. "He's the one with the red car. He was supposed to pick me up tonight, with Aaron, and…" Her voice trailed off.

"Joshua Benitez won't be coming, either," he said. "As for Aaron Soler, let's just say his plans have changed."

Girls. Pot sessions. Repeat performance. His words kept echoing in her head as she stood stock-still on the sidewalk. This time, she shivered for real. The night breeze was nothing compared to the cold coming from within her

"Did you want to sit down?" Trey moved his arm out of the way and slid to one side of the bench.

Stella hurried over and plopped down next to him, before she collapsed from the sheer weight of information she was absorbing.

"How long has this…been going on?" So many questions popped into her head, but it was difficult to put them into words. This was the kind of urban cautionary tale picked up and sensationalized by late-night crime investigation shows. "How did you know about them? How the hell do I know you're even telling the truth?"

"I don't have to answer any of that, do I?" He leaned forward, placing his elbows on his thighs and clasping his massive hands between them. He turned his head and peered at her face. "Or would you really want me to?"

She found herself looking into his eyes. They were midnight-black, unblinking. Strangely, she felt no discomfort under his gaze; instead, she stared right back.

"I just wanted to go on a date with Aaron, you know," she said softly. "When he asked me out, I was on top of the world, everyone at school was looking at me. They all saw me. And Aaron…he actually knew who I was, he got my name right and everything."

"I'm sure he did." There was no sympathy or sarcasm in his voice. He sounded as if he didn't have to convince anyone of anything. "He knew Victoria, Yasmeen, Jennifer and Grace very well, too. Unlike you, they never stood a chance."

Stella didn't know the other three, but Jennifer Ang was a sophomore Aaron had dated the previous semester. She was a beauty queen, slated to compete in the national circuit of pageants that coming summer. Shortly after Jennifer and Aaron broke up, Jennifer's parents, who both worked abroad, had pulled her out of college in the middle of the year and brought her with them to Singapore. There had been rumors of a pregnancy, a party blunder that displeased her sponsors and ruined her image, an expulsion notice that was kept quiet...

"I knew Jennifer," she said. "She's a beauty queen who used to go to my college. She was his girlfriend for a while. She left town end of last semester."

"She got lucky. Grace was from about six weeks ago; she was studying Political Science in the university across town. She sat where you are sitting now. They saw her here before she got in the car with Benitez. She's in rehab now."

The strange reality of it all was overwhelming. In a matter of hours, she had been stood up in what was supposed to be the biggest date of life, her great crush had become a junkie who was bad news for girls, and a stranger from out of nowhere had appeared to be some twisted version of a guardian angel.

"Do you know where Aaron is?"

There was a crooked smile at the corner of Trey's mouth. "Do I really have to answer that question? The less you know, the better for you."

"I can't just sit here without knowing anything," she insisted. "If you want me to at least believe in what you're trying to tell me, then give me some answers."

"Soler won't be able to come here tonight. He and his friend are both at the docks. I brought them there earlier. We're trying to get them to sing. If they're lucky, they would get a little beaten down. If not..." He shrugged. "It's not like they even cared about what would happen to those girls."

"And you...you got them there?"

"It's my job. I work for the man who decided to put them there and, at the same time, get you out of something you wouldn't want."

She sat next to him, trying to keep her breathing even. She had somehow stumbled straight into the plot of a cheap action movie. At any other time, this would have felt contrived, even cheesy.

But she felt nothing like that.

This was a close call, not a joke. She could have ended up like any of those girls.

At that moment, Stella wanted nothing more than to see her mother. If anything happened to her, she could not even imagine her mother's reaction, the pain it would cause her. Even thinking about it made her feel *guilty*.

"I think I want to go home," she said.

The intersection was almost empty except for a few pedestrians and the familiar nighttime vendors who sold peanuts, duck eggs and green mangoes from their baskets. Most of the stores were already closed for the night. She had been there for almost three hours.

"I'll walk you there." He stood up the same time she did. Side by side, she barely made it to his shoulder. "Or wait until you get into a taxi."

"That won't be necessary," she said, flustered. "I live a few blocks away, near the commercial port."

"You can walk on your own if you want. I'll follow, anyway, and make sure you get there."

At any other time, she would have found those words creepy. She would have felt uncomfortable at the very least.

Tonight, however, was the kind of night that brought creepy to shame. If anything, she was past creepy.

With Trey, there was no feeling of discomfort, only a sense of awareness that he was more intimidating than everyone and everything else around her.

"Fine," she said, thinking she would rather have someone like him walking her home, rather than the less impressive assurance provided by her box cutter. "Let's go."

Criminal

She looked at the sky again, maybe for the seventh time in the past half hour.

It was still raining. It showed no signs of letting up.

Stella stood by the waiting shed next to the main gate of her college. She was still mercifully dry, if not for errant drops of rainwater, brought about by nasty gusts of wind, whipping against her skin and her white college uniform.

This wasn't rain, she thought. This was a full-blown storm, at least Signal Number Two.

Night had been upon them for hours, with clouds blotting out the sun since mid-afternoon. All the classes for the evening finished at seven-thirty. It was already past eight.

The campus would be locked up soon. She would have to brave the storm on foot and wade her way through the flooded streets if she didn't want to get kicked out or get stuck. It was only a matter of time before the water levels got too high, if the rain didn't stop.

It was a simple, straightforward plan. Out the school and through the city's main street, where there was better drainage. She could use the buildings as shelter and sprint the last few hundred meters home past the plaza and the church. She would be soaked to the bone and maybe even get sick, but at least she wouldn't freeze to death outside her own school.

She turned to the other students huddled next to her, looking them over as she took off her shoes. There were three other girls and two boys, all looking as if they had the same predicament as she: brave the rain and flood, or wait it out. Her own choice already decided, she put her shoes in her bag and gave them a silent nod before walking out into the downpour.

It was easy enough to cross the road and make her way past the market. She was able to take shelter in the windows and awnings, up to and until she reached the main street.

By the time she made it to the intersection, the rain was so heavy she could barely see past a few steps in front of her. The shops had closed, with most of their lights and signs put out. What little light there was came from the streetlamps that still worked. She could feel water, cold and sticky, running in quick tiny currents under her feet. Blasted on all sides by strong winds, she could barely stay upright. It was like being in the middle of a sunken, vengeful city.

So much for her plan of using the buildings as shelter. She'd be lucky if she could make it past this junction. One wrong step could lead her into an open drainage hatch, if she didn't fall on her face, drown or get electrocuted first.

She stood in front of the sixty-year-old grocery store, squinting through the rain at a dim light coming from the window of a single shop across the street.

It was the old couple's leather repair shop. Were they still there? Could she possibly stay with them until this was over? Could she even cover that much ground without dying along the way?

Throwing caution literally to the winds, she drew her bag tighter against her body and sprinted full speed across the darkened road. Her bare feet burned from the roughness of the asphalt and the icy coldness of the flood.

"Hello? Can I please come in?" she called out, half-crashing, half-stumbling against the shop entrance. She pushed the wooden door open with all her strength and promptly ran into a wall.

She felt the wall give way a little, then something grabbed her upper arms, steadying her. It took her a second to figure out that she had run into someone, not something.

"Stella?"

It took a few more seconds for her eyes to adjust to the soft yellowish light inside the shop. Through a haze of stinging rainwater, she could make out a large black figure with equally dark hair and eyes. His face was the last thing that came into focus.

It was him.

"Trey?"

"What the hell are you doing here? Are you okay?"

She flinched at the harshness of his voice, or maybe at the strength of the grip he had on her. She could barely move her upper body.

At least she could still move her head. She nodded. "I'm fine. Can you please let go of me?"

His hands loosened and fell away. She watched him take a step back, inwardly debating with herself whether or not this was all real.

"Did I hurt you?" Without taking his eyes off her, he picked up something from the front counter. It was an emergency lantern, the source of light she had seen through the window. The shadows in the room shifted as he brought the lantern overhead.

"No, it's okay," she replied, a little too aware of how closely they stood to each other. The repair shop had always been tiny, but now it felt considerably cramped and tight. "Where's Auntie Yolly and Uncle Frank?"

"They've gone home. Did you come here to see them? All

the shops closed hours ago." There was a note of disbelief in his voice.

She shook her head. "I was going to take shelter here. It was the only place with the lights on. I thought I could get home on foot, but the streets are too badly flooded."

Exhaustion and cold started nipping at her joints. She leaned against the wooden counter and put her bag on top. Her uniform was drenched, the skirt stained by the flood waters.

It was only then that she noticed it.

The blood.

Next to the space where she had put her bag, she spied small streaks of dark red liquid. Her eyes followed the stains over the side, all the way down the floor, to the spot where Auntie Yolly would usually stand to serve customers. Concealed behind the wooden counter were two limp bodies leaning against each other, their faces split open like overripe watermelons.

She screamed.

She tried but never got the chance. He put his arm around her and brought her close to him, pressing her so tightly against his body that any sound she could make was muffled against his chest.

"Stella," he said, very calmly, almost soothingly. "Stella. Stella, look at me. Please don't scream. Just look at me."

She could feel her body shake violently at the gory sight she had just witnessed. She focused on his voice, the welcome heat of his body. She was fine. It was just blood. It wasn't her blood.

"Look at me, Stella," he repeated. "Don't scream. They're not dead. I won't hurt you."

Clutching at his shirt, she willed herself to open her eyes.

She could see, under the light of the lantern he held up, that he was looking at her, too, into her eyes. His own eyes smoldered like hot coals. She focused on them. He wouldn't hurt her.

"Good," he said. "Now breathe."

She breathed out, a long exhale that made her light-headed. She held on to him, kept her eyes locked onto the somehow comforting familiarity of his face, as she tried to get her bearings.

"Please get me out of here," she heard herself say, trying very hard not to think of the bloody pulps next to her.

His face impassive, he let go of her and moved to the entrance to bolt it shut from the inside. When he was done, he gestured for her to go further inside the shop. "Let's go upstairs. If the water gets any higher, we'll be safer there."

Still feeling sick to her stomach, Stella carefully took her bag and did as instructed. Beyond the front of the shop, behind a thin plastic curtain, was the small workroom she was familiar with, lined wall to wall with tools and Uncle Frank's ancient pedal machine. To one side was a narrow flight of steps.

Guided by the light of the lantern, she was able to find her way to the mezzanine in record time. It was no larger than the downstairs area but had a higher ceiling. It appeared to be some kind of storage room for the shop's supplies. At one end of the room was a large glass window.

She put her bag on a shelf and made her way to the window. There was almost nothing to see, except the rain pelting against the glass and a very limited view of the flooded street outside. Most of the working streetlamps she saw earlier had gone out.

"You should sit down." Trey had put down the lamp on a tiny table and was bringing over a wooden stool for her. "You didn't have to see what you just saw. I guess you'd want an explanation?"

She settled on the stool, stretching out her legs and bare feet. She looked at him as he backed up and settled his large frame on the table next to the lamp. He looked bigger than she remembered; his hair was longer, too.

It didn't surprise her that he was talking so casually about the scene downstairs.

"Did you do that to them?" she asked, boldly.

"I did, just before you got here," he answered. "As I said, they're not dead. They're just out. I remember doing the same thing to your old friends a while back."

She remembered that night vividly. After she'd reached home, she had looked over her shoulder to see Trey gone. She had tried not to think about what had happened and had not told anyone, not even her mother. In the Monday that followed, there had been a large ruckus at the college about the two boys and the rest of their circle getting arrested. None of their gang of nine ever made it back to campus. As far as she'd heard, the other boys had been caught in the act of using drugs and hurting girls from other schools. Stella had thought that maybe Joshua had sung a little too well, or maybe Trey and his boss had made him do so.

"What did they do this time? Drugs?" Stella tried not to think of all the blood splattered on the counter and the floor.

"They were going to burn this building down. They got into the shop by breaking the front lock. They probably wanted to make it look like an accident that started from here, with the amount of leather oil they were carrying. They could have easily taken out this entire block, too. These buildings may look like solid stone from the outside, but inside it's all old wood."

"Why would they want to do that?" She thought of all the people who had stores in the block. She had known most of them since she was little; if not by name, she recognized them by face.

"Territory. Those fuckers are not from here, they're not even from Visayas. They're the Zamora family from Manila. They want to control the Pier District, starting with the small businesses. With the livelihood of the people gone, it would be easier to buy them out."

Trey got off the table and walked the length of the room to look out the window himself. "They tried the same thing last month at the port, with the vendor stalls. We barely got there on time. Otherwise, they could have burned down nearly two hundred stalls and parts of the commercial port."

She lived there. Her house was a stone's throw away from those stalls. She used to eat there regularly. "The only thing I heard about the port was that there was a huge riot that broke out among drunks over videoke. It was all over the news last month. My mother warned me not to go there in the evenings once they start all the singing and drinking."

He looked over his shoulder at her. "It was a good story, wasn't it? The boys staged the riot so well and got all the attention. We were lucky at the time."

She hesitated before asking her next question. "What are you going to do about them?" She gestured vaguely downwards.

"We're tracking down their friends who could be in the other buildings. As soon as we could get through the flood, we're taking these sons of bitches to their quarters across town. It took us a while to find out where they're holed up. Turns out they live in the house of Greg Garces. He's got ties with the Filipino-American mafia. I wouldn't be surprised if he's the one funding this little takeover attempt."

Another cause, another enemy.

More blood.

Why Trey did what he was doing she had no idea. "What do they want from the Pier District? I've lived here all my life. Most of us in our neighborhood have. It's just boats and warehouses and shops, and tiny old houses like mine."

He turned to face her completely. "Whoever controls the district controls the shipping routes and traffic. What goes in, what goes out, what everybody does in it. Most importantly, who gets to do business. All kinds of business."

"Somebody already does that, right?" She searched her memory for the name. It was a very old name, the elusive but notorious family that owned at least half of the district where she lived. "The Esguerras?"

"Raphael Esguerra. Ever since he took over a few years ago,

other families and groups have been trying to take him down on all sides. A new leader usually takes a lot of heat. We've been putting out fires for a while now."

"You do dangerous things" she said. "You could get killed. Can't you just…quit?"

"And do what?"

"I don't know. Live and work somewhere else."

"Some of us can't just quit," he said with more emotion than she'd ever heard. "Some of us can't just give up the life we were born into. I grew up in the docks. I've lived here my whole life, too, just like you. I will do everything in my power to keep the Pier District from getting destroyed by outsiders, even if it means becoming a criminal to get rid of the people in my way."

His eyes left her then, as he focused his attention back to the window.

She stood up and picked her way over to the window, to see what he was looking at. It was still windy and raining heavily.

"I hope it stops raining soon. I want to go home. I've been at school since eight this morning."

"Aren't you cold? You look like you're going to be sick soon." The concern on his face made her aware of their closeness.

All she had to do was reach out, to touch him, to make sure he was real.

Ever since that night at the intersection, she had thought about him constantly, wondering if he ever existed at all. She had wanted to ask others about him, but had decided not to. She knew if he'd been just a figment of her imagination she would be devastated.

She was soaked with rainwater and freezing all the way to her insides. She wasn't even aware she had wrapped her own arms around her body to keep herself warm.

"I'm fine. It was my fault. I forgot my umbrella at the library. By the time I came back to get it, I was too late."

"Here." Trey started unbuttoning his shirt. She stared, heat rushing to her face. She tried to move her legs, to step away from him, but she was frozen to the spot. His black shirt opened, showing a grey t-shirt underneath. He took off the polo and handed it to her. "Put this on."

She was blushing and she knew it. The grey shirt had a tighter fit on his body. His shoulders and chest were broad, contrasting with his flat stomach and narrow hips. His black polo ended up in her shaky hand.

"Thanks," she heard herself choke out.

"I'm sorry if there are any…stains on it. I don't have anything warmer."

His shirt was the warmest thing she had ever touched. It had a clean, fresh scent, something like pine, tinged with the sea. She slid her arms into the shirt, almost disappearing into its considerably larger size.

"It's fine. It's very warm. Thank you."

They both stood by the window in silence, staring out into the rain and the nearly invisible city street.

"How are you, Stella?" It had gotten so quiet, his voice almost startled her. "I didn't get to ask you earlier."

"Life goes on, I suppose," she said. "School has been busier since I was a freshman. Thankfully, no one tried anything since that night. I think everyone got a little bit scared with what happened to Aaron and Joshua."

"A little bit scared?"

"Scared shitless, then?"

"Better."

She smiled. "So, how are you?"

He held up his left hand to the light. His knuckles looked freshly skinned, with a little blood caked and dried on them. "Bloody after my little fun. I guess I'm fine."

She was tempted to reach out and touch his hand. She could only clench her own fingers into a tight fist.

"I don't think I ever got to say thank you," she said.

"For what?"

"For back then." She could feel herself blushing again. She really had to get herself under control. All this caused by someone she barely knew, someone who had the knack of appearing out of the darkness for her, whenever she needed it most. "And for now, I think."

He shook his head. "You're thanking me for showing you two half-dead bodies in a leather repair shop?"

"For being there, Trey. It means something to me, even if the thought had never crossed your mind. Don't be like that."

She was rewarded with the tiniest of smiles. "This is as much of a surprise to me as it is to you, Stella."

The moment was interrupted by his phone ringing. He took it out of his pocket and answered. "Yes. I'm still here. Are you sure there's no one else out there?"

Trey looked out the window again. "Can you drop someone off first, then come back? Good."

"There's a car on the way," he said to her, replacing the phone in his pocket. "It can get through the flood. They'll take you home."

"That's great. Thanks." She looked around her, never at him. He would disappear again for goodness knew how long. She had to say it. "Will I see you again?"

He was already making his way back to retrieve the lamp from the table. He stopped mid-step and stared at her from over his shoulder. "What?"

"Will I ever get to see you again?" she repeated, as bravely as she could.

"Why would you want to see me? People don't usually like seeing me."

"I like seeing you," she retorted.

"Give me your phone." He walked back to her and held out

his hand.

She reached into her bag, between rows of damp notebooks, and retrieved her phone. It was only slightly damp on the outside. The tiny device almost disappeared into his hand.

He looked at her phone's casing for a few seconds. It was made of shiny white silicone, decorated with a stylized drawing of a black archangel. He didn't comment. He turned it over to the screen side and started typing.

She heard his phone ringing again. "That's you calling. I'll save your number. Call me whenever you need, okay? I will answer."

She was tempted to say something in response when he handed the phone back to her. Nothing came out of her mouth. Not even when she retrieved her bag and followed him down the stairs.

She stood as close as she possibly could to the entrance, the farthest from the two bodies behind the counter. Trey was talking on his phone again, to someone else, about meeting them in another district across town.

It barely took any time before the car reached the flooded main street. She saw its headlights approaching and turned to him.

Stella finally found her voice. "Thanks." She took off his shirt and handed it back.

He shook his head. "No, keep it."

"I don't think I can." *Even if she wanted to.* "My mother will ask a lot of questions. It's a very small house. And it's just the two of us."

"Don't worry. I understand." He took the shirt and put it back on just as she heard a muted honking from outside. He unlocked the shop's front door and held it open for her. "Take care of yourself."

"You, too." She walked past him and stepped back into the street. Once outside, she could see that the rain had calmed down. It was still pouring heavily, but she could barely feel the wind.

He followed her. "Tell Mario where you want to go. He'll drive you there."

A dark four-wheel drive had stopped outside the shop. It stood amidst the flood looking like a tank. A middle-aged man rolled down the window by the driver's side and was about to step out when Trey held up a hand and opened the backseat door himself.

"Good night, Stella." The rain dripped on his face and hair. He didn't even blink.

She finally reached out and got to touch his left hand, the one with the skinned knuckles. It felt warm, rough, strong. "Thanks again. Good night."

He nodded and shut the car door. He didn't move from the spot where he stood, not even when the giant car pulled out of the sidewalk and started making its way through the flood.

She never took her eyes off him. Not until the sight of him was swallowed by the darkness that stretched out behind her.

Farewell

She looked up at the sky, then down at her watch. She sighed, trying to find a more comfortable position on the bench. Her legs and feet, clad in the black regulation stockings and low-heeled shoes of her school uniform, felt cramped. She felt warm in the white suit and regretted not changing into something cooler.

In the early evening, the intersection was the same as always, bright, messy and full of people rushing to catch a ride or selling food and trinkets. There was a thick, balmy breeze coming from the nearby waters of the docks, heavily tinged with salt. It was going to be a humid night.

Was it only a few years ago that she had sat on this same bench, shivering in a white cardigan, grappling with the dark realities of the world she was growing up in? It felt like a lifetime ago.

She wasn't surprised when someone suddenly took the spot next to her on the bench. She kind of expected it.

Stella had expected anything to happen since she got the text message from Trey last week. She had never called or messaged him in the past eighteen months since they last saw each other.

She had not deleted his number, either.

It was the only message she had ever received from him.

She had called him back straightaway, just to make sure it wasn't someone else messing with her. He had answered after two rings, in that deep, raspy voice that sometimes followed her, especially when she walked alone in the city streets at night. Sometimes she dreamt of that voice, too.

For this Friday, she skipped her last class and told her friends she would meet them at the movies tomorrow evening. She had the foolproof reason of completing a report due that Monday.

"Hi, Stella." Trey, no longer a disembodied presence at the back of her head, looked surprisingly different. His long hair was tied back in a neat ponytail; he was dressed in a green polo shirt, blue jeans and brown shoes. He looked almost normal; his scarred face was as fierce-looking as ever, maybe even a little sharper with age.

Stella wondered how he thought she looked. She had definitely gotten taller since last time. Over the past few years, it was her height that brought her attention and sometimes opportunities neither she nor her mother had ever expected. A few months ago, she was approached by an events company to model for a local fashion show early next year.

"How are you, Trey?" she asked, politely. Light conversation had never been part of their interactions.

His Adam's apple was bobbing up and down. "I'm fine. Thanks for coming. I didn't think you would even answer my text. How have you been?"

She forced a smile, as strange as it felt to have normal small talk with him. "Good. Busy. Reports and exams take up most of my time. I'll be graduating this school year."

There was a rustle as he pulled out something from behind his back. She was certain he had gotten even bigger since last time; his shoulders looked wider in the more flattering cut and color of his shirt.

To her surprise, there was a small box of roses in his hands. There were three: one red, one pink and one white.

"I didn't know which color you liked, but I took a chance and picked roses," he said. "You always have on some kind of cologne that smells like roses."

"Yes, I like roses," she answered, taken aback. "Roses are nice."

If she had to list a hundred things this man was capable of doing, giving her roses would never even be a remote consideration, much less knowing how she actually smelled.

She reached out to take the box, trying to think of something else to say and failing miserably. She wasn't sure if she had intended to touch him, but her hands landed on top of his.

She looked up into his dark eyes and, sure enough, they were on her, too. She understood that look from a man, far better now than she did four years ago. No matter how mysterious he appeared to be, he was still a man, wasn't he?

"I wanted to see you," he finally said, breaking the silent, unmoving exchange between them. "I didn't want to leave town without telling you."

Her fingers closed around the box. It was made of white cardboard, plain yet sturdy, with a plastic display window to showcase the flowers inside. It was something she expected from someone like him: unadorned and straightforward.

"Where are you going?"

"Does it matter?"

"It does to me." She clutched the box closer to her, pressing it to the space between her chest and her stomach.

"I'm going to get a few things out of the way. North, mostly in Manila. We've lost a lot of good people to the Zamoras this past year. They haven't stopped trying to take over the Pier District."

His back heaved in what looked like a sigh. "It's only a matter of time before this escalates to an all-out war. But Iloilo is our home, we were born and raised here. We won't give it up, so we're bringing the war to them."

He was bringing the war to them, she thought.

Stella suddenly felt cold, empty, abandoned. The same way she had felt the first time she met him, on this very bench.

"You'll be back, right? You said before this is the life you were born into. You can't just leave, can you?"

There was that familiar tiny smile at the corner of his mouth. "It's not about leaving or staying. When I chose to do this, I knew I wouldn't be coming back. Sometimes, there are things we need to do that we can't just walk away from."

"I see," she said, evenly. "You'll be missing my graduation, then." It sounded stupid and pointless, but nothing ever made sense with him anyway. She could not even fathom how deep, dark and bloody the world he lived in was.

"I guess I will."

"I was a freshman when we first met, you know."

He nodded. "So, are you going to the senior prom with someone special?"

"Prom?" she echoed. "I haven't really thought about it. I don't have a special someone."

The idea had never really crossed her mind, not since what happened during freshman year. She had nothing against boys in general, but since then she had been averse to the young adult rituals of courting and dating.

Sure, there were a few boys who showed interest, some more than others. Darryl, whose family moved from another province at the start of their junior year, had been courting her shortly after he completed his first semester at the college. He was part of the student council and tutored younger students in Math subjects. Her mother liked him immensely. Stella didn't exactly dislike him; she just wasn't interested.

"It took me a while to trust boys again, after what happened. But I've learned a thing or two since then. I would stick an idiot in the throat with a box cutter before they could try anything funny." She had to smile through the heaviness in her muscles, a strange sensation considering how empty she felt inside.

They sat in silence for a while, before he stood up.

"I'm glad you're okay, Stella. At least I got one thing right in all of this."

Driven by a sudden sense of panic, she jumped to her own feet. "Are you going now?" she blurted out.

"I'm leaving tomorrow morning, so I'd better get ready." He was looking down at her with his mouth in a thin line. "I'm sorry if I bothered or upset you in any way. If there was someone I had to say goodbye to, it was you."

She felt something rise in her throat, bitter and painful and stinging hot.

Goodbye, she thought. It sounded so final and absolute.

Guardian angels were supposed to stay, weren't they? Wasn't he supposed to stay with her?

"I'm glad you told me," she said honestly. "It gave me a chance to see you. I thought I'd see you again sooner, after last time. But I'm glad you're here now."

"Me, too."

She swallowed hard, trying her best to stem the flood rising dangerously fast from within her. "It's early. I skipped my last class to meet you."

Before he could respond, she continued. "Let's eat something, okay? It will be my treat. I never had the chance to do anything for you."

Without giving him the opportunity to refuse, she grabbed him by the arm and pulled him through the throng of people milling the busy nighttime streets. She knew this place was part of him. This was home for Trey.

They had dinner of grilled fish and rice at a small, open-air eatery on the docks. It was nice to see him doing something normal with her, for a change.

Or for the last time.

It was almost nine in the evening when the lights of the stores and restaurants started going out, signaling the end of the day. She thought back to the time she had sat at the intersection and looked at the dying stars as her own hopes died, too.

Trey was the only constant presence between then and now, between an innocent teenager's disappointment and her first real heartbreak.

Her twisted kind of guardian angel, who was leaving her life as soon as the day was over. She was determined not to lose any more time she had left with this beguiling man.

"You live near here, don't you?" She had her hand on his arm, a gesture she had dared to try earlier, as they walked on the open pier, the area where smaller passenger boats docked in the daytime. She had thought he would not want to be touched, but she was wrong. She was glad to be wrong.

"It's near the old Customs office," he said, a little too formally, nodding towards a cluster of warehouses a block away. "My boss bought a few buildings here to keep some of the cars and for us to stay in if we wanted. I didn't want to live out of town."

"Can I see your place?" Heat flooded her face at her own boldness.

He stopped in his tracks. "It's late. I should be walking you home.

"I don't want to go home. Not yet."

"What do you want, then, Stella?"

Before her mind realized what she was doing, her body and heart had already made the call.

Her school bag, with his gift of roses, slid off her shoulder as she let go of his arm to, finally, put her own arms around him. She could reach his shoulders, his neck; she had to stand on tiptoes and force his head down with all her might. And it worked.

She kissed him.

Reckoning

She didn't think about it anymore. She just moved as she had always wanted to. She ran her hands over his back and his thick hair; she used her tongue to taste him, his lips, the inside of his mouth. The rest of her followed; her chest and her hips pressed against him, wanting more, maybe at least for him to touch her, too.

He understood.

She knew as much when he came to life, knowing exactly what she wanted, what she needed.

His lips moved against hers; his tongue was deliciously soft and snake-like as it twisted its way into the depths of her mouth. His hands were all over her. His fingers ran through her long hair, his palms burned a path through her skin as he wrapped his arms around her waist and started caressing her buttocks. It wasn't very long until she was pressed against him so tightly, she could feel him, hard and insistent, against her own softness. His fingertips glided inside her skirt as he lifted one of her legs to wrap around his hip.

She gasped when he touched that part of her, expertly reaching inside the modest underwear she wore with her school uniform. His fingers rubbed and stroked her as she moaned against his chest.

She denied herself the pleasure that was beginning to build and decided to come back up for air. She grabbed at his arms, still feeling him against her.

"Take me home, Trey," she whispered into the night. "Make me yours."

He was always more at ease in the shadows. She watched as he picked up her things with ruthless efficiency. This time, it was his turn to take her hand and lead the way.

He lived in a warehouse, one filled with auto parts. The lighting was sparse; except for a few fluorescent bulbs, it was the lights of the pier that danced with the shadows. He locked the door behind him and led her to a tiny corner where stood a small table, a portable chest of plastic drawers, a tiny refrigerator, and his bed, wooden, with a thin mattress on top.

He did not say anything; neither did she. He brought her to the bed and made her stand before him. He undressed her then, unbuttoning her blouse and skirt first and sliding them off of her. He fumbled a bit with her bra, but when he finally undid the clasp and took it off, she blushed deeply as he brought his lips to her nipples and suckled them hungrily. She would have fallen to the floor, easily, had it not been for his firm grip around her body.

When he was done, he lowered her stockings and panties and, before she could protest, his lips, his tongue and his hands were on her, all over her. After a few moments, he lifted her to the bed, settling her gently on her back. His mouth came down between her legs again, as did his fingers, and she was at his mercy. She called his name, bucked her hips, spread herself further, dug her nails into his shoulders, until he brought her to the peak and she heard herself scream and moan in pleasure.

"You are so beautiful." She heard him speak huskily, from somewhere above her. It took a few seconds for her eyes to focus as she came down from what she knew was her first climax. She had read about it in romance novels, seen it in movies that made her blush, and even heard girls with boyfriends talk about it, but she had never expected it to feel like this.

She had never expected she would feel it with him.

In what little light there was, she could see him next to her on the bed, his dark eyes almost disappearing into the shadows. He was still fully clothed.

"Oh." Embarrassment sank in for the first time. Her hands came up, to cover her utter lack of modesty, but his fingertips were on her face before she could reach for something, like a blanket or pillow, to cover up with.

"You don't have to hide. Never from me." For the first time, she heard a tremble in his voice. She could barely see his face. His fingertips were gentle as he traced her cheeks; the skin on his hands was hard, rough and warm. She could smell herself in his touch.

She reached for him. Before she could wrap her arms around him again, he caught her wrists.

"I think it's time for you to go home." There it was again, the shakiness in his voice. "I'll walk you there." He slowly let her go.

"No," she said, trying to lift her torso, to get a better look at him. "I want to stay with you."

He hesitated, then sat up, the cot creaking under his weight. "This is your…first time, isn't it?"

"Yes." Was there something she had done he didn't like? "What does that have to do with anything?"

"This is the biggest mistake you could ever make." His back was as stiff and unyielding as a mountain, his voice low and almost menacing.

"Mistake? Who made you responsible for my decisions?" Heat rushed to her cheeks and forehead. She grabbed at the thin striped blanket folded under the pillow she had been lying on and hastily wrapped it around her nakedness.

"Decision? You call this a decision? To sleep with me?"

"To be with you, Trey." She was close to tears. She slid off the bed and got to her feet. He still had his back turned to her. At least he couldn't see her so disheveled and hurt. "I want to be with you. It was my choice to make. Don't you dare tell me you didn't want it, too. I felt it. Don't you fucking dare deny it."

He put his hands on his thick legs and rose, almost painstakingly. "I'm not denying anything." He turned slowly, running his fingers through his hair, which had become half-unbound after their kisses. He kept his eyes hooded, gaze to the floor, or at least not on her.

"I've never wanted a woman as much as I want you. Look at you, Stella. How could I or any man say no to you?"

"Then don't."

"If only it were that simple. If only I were any other man."

"You will never be any other man," she said, almost impatiently. "Look at you, Trey. How could any man compare to you?"

"Any other man wouldn't leave you." It was almost a whisper.

That stopped her.

"Then come back." Her lips finally uttered the very thing her heart had known for a long time. "When all this is over, come back to me."

As soon as she finished saying the words, a lone tear slid down the corner of her left eye, landing and splashing on her naked shoulder. She was terrified he saw it.

That was the last shred of her dignity.

Somehow, that was also the last shred of his control.

As long as it took her to blink back more tears, he closed the distance between them. The way he grabbed hold of her around the waist was almost bone-breaking, crushing the breath out of her. His lips came down on hers like a clap of thunder, as powerful and overwhelming as he.

Her flimsy cover of a blanket fell to the floor, just as she gave him her complete surrender. This time, there was no waiting, no caressing, no gentleness, as she kissed him back like a woman starved.

Dimly, she felt her hands rip away at the last barriers between them, his clothing. It didn't take long for him to be just as naked as she. He looked beautifully inhuman in the dim light and shifting shadows; his skin was smooth where there were no scars, but he had dozens of them all over his body, mixed with what looked and felt like burn marks. His hair fell on her face like a velvet curtain, scented by the sea and his sweat.

They didn't even make it to the bed, or at least she did, halfway. He was inside her, a perfect fit, buried completely, as her legs went around his waist, his shadow looming over her. She felt him thrusting faster and harder by the second, heard him say her name again and again, and, finally, asked her to look at him.

Their eyes locked briefly, and she drowned at the ferocity and desire she saw in the way he looked at her, and his lips were on hers again. He thrust the hardest then, and he shouted as his body shook as if he had a hundred earthquakes inside him, from inside her.

He collapsed, draped across her, his hair and sweat and breath on her breasts. She could feel a slick wetness burning straight from him into her.

Her heart was pounding so loudly she could barely hear anything else. She put her arms around him and kissed the top of his head, feeling only tenderness as she watched him looking spent and vulnerable.

Is this how it was supposed to feel?

She never had any more time to think about it that night. She could only feel, only him. They made love again, and again, and once more. He was insatiable, as if he wanted every last part of her for himself, but, to her surprise, so was she.

By dawn, he had touched and kissed every inch of her, and she of him. She was straddling him, arms around his neck, his teeth and tongue on her nipples, when she saw the first strains of light filter in through the high windows of the warehouse. By the time she came in his embrace, moaning his name, morning was upon them.

He was on his back and she sprawled on top of him, nuzzling his chest, when she realized it was the first time she was seeing him in the light of day.

"Come back to me, Trey," she blurted out, afraid he would somehow disappear. "No matter what happens, just come back to me."

He didn't respond, not for a long time. His arms went around her, so tightly, so protectively. She felt his lips on her temple, his heartbeat in her ear, his hands in her hair. She took these in, every touch, every scent, every sound, every feeling.

"I love you, Stella," he finally said.

I love you.

After he said the words, he slowly moved her to the bed and wrapped her in his blanket. She watched him dress in his usual dark clothing and take only a black backpack.

"It's yours now," he said, giving her the keys he had used the night before. "Do whatever you like."

Before she could protest, he brought his arms around her and kissed her deeply. With one last caress on her cheek and her hair, he was gone.

Trey.

She didn't even know his last name.

Stella got out of his bed, dressed and gathered her things. It was only when she finished locking up the warehouse that she felt the scalding pain in her throat, from last night, finally bubble to the surface, unleashing itself with her tears.

As she walked home, she didn't have the heart to check her phone, knowing that it was probably bursting with worried texts and missed calls from her mother. She would deal with it all later. All that mattered at the moment was she make it through the pain, see herself home alive.

She had no idea how hard she had been clutching his box of roses in her hands. She was just about to cross the intersection when it fell from her grasp. The box burst open, spilling the three roses onto the street, along with a small rectangle of paper.

She crouched down and slowly gathered the fallen items, fitting them into her school bag, feeling spent and raw as she did. The rectangle turned out to be a business card, with something written on the back of it by hand. The name was familiar.

RAPHAEL I. ESGUERRA, III
Chief Executive Officer
Esguerra Holdings

Trey's boss. There was a number printed underneath, which looked oddly familiar. It took her a few seconds to figure out that the mobile phone number was Trey's. She had looked at his number and only message from last week so many times.

Why was his phone number on his boss' card?

At the back of the paper, in bold, slashing handwriting, was a short message.

Call whenever you need.
There will be an answer.
Trey

Unable to make sense of what she had just read, she fumbled with the rest of her things and slowly sat down at the bench by the intersection, taking deep breaths.

She slowly went back in memory, to what he had said in the time she was with him.

"Iloilo is our home, we were born and raised here. We won't give it up, so we're bringing the war to them."

"I work for the man who decided to put them there and, at the same time, get you out of something you wouldn't want."

"When I chose to do this, I knew I wouldn't be coming back."

"Some of us can't just quit. Some of us can't just give up the life we were born into."

Was Trey the boss he was referring to? Was he actually Raphael Esguerra?

Was he the Raphael Esguerra who protected her city?

Unable to stop herself, she took out her phone. The screen showed eighteen missed calls and almost double in unread messages. The battery was down to twelve percent. She scrolled through her contacts, found Trey's number, and called it. She felt an icy chill envelop her body, despite the warmth of the morning sun.

Her call was picked up after two rings.

"Hello, Miss Montero. Good morning." The voice was different, older, female. It sounded almost like her own mother's voice.

"Hello," Stella echoed. She suddenly felt disoriented. "Who's this? Is Trey there?"

"My name is Rhoda, Miss Montero. I work for Mister Esguerra. Is there something I can do for you?"

"Where's Trey? I want to talk to him. Please."

"I believe he has informed you he will be indisposed. He has given us instructions to be at your service, as and when you need."

Us? Her brain tried to cope with the words of the woman at the other end of the line. *At her service?*

Wherever Trey was, she had already gotten her answer.

"No, thanks," she heard herself say. "I just wanted to give him back the keys to his... house."

"Did you? I was under the impression he has given them to you, to access and use the warehouse as you please."

"No. Yes. I didn't understand what he was trying to tell me."

There was a pause from Rhoda. "Is there anything else you need, Miss Montero? I can send a car for you if you need to get somewhere, wherever you are in the city."

To her horror, Stella felt a few tears slowly escape her already stinging, sleepless eyes. "I don't need a car. I'll walk home."

"Very well, Miss Montero. Please call me if you need anything, anything at all."

"Goodbye, Rhoda." Stella disconnected the call. She mechanically picked up her bag and stood up. She could feel her legs extend unwillingly, still sore from her night with him. She was beyond tired.

Raphael Esguerra.

A powerful name, feared and respected in the world she lived in.

Trey.

The man who moved in and out of the shadows and into her life, into her darkest dreams and desires.

They were the same person. The only man she had given her heart and her body to.

She would have given anything to make him stay. She knew, however, that no one could tell someone like Raphael Esguerra what to do.

The very same person who told her he loved her.

She had never said she loved him, too, had she? Loved him the moment she first laid eyes on him all those years ago, stepping out of the darkness, under the bright neon lights of a street corner.

It was the only regret she had. It was a prison she willingly put her heart into.

She carried this regret in the days, weeks and months that followed, silently, guardedly.

When she reached home that Saturday morning, instead of

greeting her with panic or anger, her mother told her that she received a visitor named Rhoda, the mother of one of Stella's classmates, earlier that morning. Rhoda had apologized for not calling to tell her that Stella was helping her daughter with an urgent term paper, help given at the last minute to a desperate classmate. After breakfast in a fast food restaurant with her daughter, Stella would be home.

She went to the movies that evening with her friends. On Monday, the student council started putting up posters for the senior prom, scheduled on Valentine's Day. She wasn't surprised to get asked by Darryl, whom she politely turned down. In the weeks that followed, she refused four more invitations.

It was almost Christmas when she first heard about it on the news.

It was hard to miss. A large explosion in Sampaloc, Manila had taken down almost four blocks of factories and warehouses. A hundred injured, twenty dead. Up to and until Christmas, there were interviews of a bereaved widow named Connie Zamora, clutching a brood of four children, mourning the death of her husband, business magnate Michael Zamora. Connie demanded justice for her family and the families of their employees.

The media and the police suspected terrorists trying to make a statement. Stella always looked at the sketches released to the public, but never found one she recognized.

Over the school break that December, just before New Year, she went back to the warehouse, on a quiet weekday evening.

It was the same way she had left it. She tidied up the bed, willing herself not to think of the person she had shared it with, and stripped the sheets for washing. She went through the plastic drawers and the refrigerator. The fridge had a few bottles of water and an unopened Snickers chocolate bar. The drawers contained an assortment of black and grey shirts, a few pairs of dark jeans, and shorts of different colors. All the clothes had been washed and neatly folded. In the bottom drawer was a plain ruled notebook and a few pencils. Nothing was written inside the notebook; there were only sketches that filled the pages, drawn in a neat, meticulous hand.

They were all sketches of her.

She spent the next hour crying on his bare mattress.

In January, she walked the runway for the first time, in a Dinagyang Festival fashion show. The designer was so impressed that she offered to design Stella's gown for the latter's senior prom, as part of her Valentine's Day portfolio.

February came with typhoons, one after the other. The rain on Valentine's Day reminded Stella of that night two years ago when the city was flooded.

The prom was at a seaside resort across town, in a covered pavilion with tall, thick glass windows that overlooked the beach. In spite of the weather, almost all her classmates and their dates had come.

Stella arrived with two other senior girls who didn't have escorts like her. All three of them lived in the same area and had opted to travel to and from the event together.

She made a stop at the bathroom before entering the venue. Pictures of the night were very important, according to the designer. They had contracted one of the prom photographers to take additional photos of her wearing the new dress.

The gown was made of deep red velvet, the color of blood. The neckline was cut low, off the shoulders, with small crisscrossing straps around her upper arms. The rest of the fabric was molded to her bodice and hips, then came apart by her left thigh in a slit, showing off her long legs, with the hemline almost brushing the floor.

The hairdresser had styled her hair half down, half up. It fell in waves all the way to the middle of her bare back. She had asked for three small roses to be put around the loose ponytail on top of her head. One red, one pink, one white.

'I love you, Stella.'

The words had echoed in her mind, heart and soul countless

times since she heard them, for the first, only and, possibly, last time.

Staring back at her in the mirror was the very image of a romantic heroine, draped in the colors of love.

But she wasn't that heroine.

She was Stella Montero, who didn't even have a date to the prom. She didn't have someone special. She already had something more than that.

She already had her prison.

Storm

The prom was meant to last past midnight. The weather had other plans.

At nearly eleven that evening, Stella stood next to the glass door of the pavilion and looked up. She couldn't see any of the stars. The sky was almost completely covered in thick clouds. There was only the moon, cutting through the dark shroud with tiny yet sharp slivers of light.

The rain fell in a steady downpour, the winds picking up in speed with each hour that passed. A full-blown storm would be upon them soon.

She had spent the past few hours having her picture taken and getting congratulated by practically everyone present: her teachers, classmates and schoolmates, even visitors from other schools. She was, apparently, the frontrunner for Prom Queen.

She was not surprised when someone from the student council came over to escort her across the dance floor. It was the treasurer, a classmate of hers since freshman year named Vic. He guided her up the small stage and led her to a spot in a line where three other girls stood. Vic winked at her and mouthed, *"Congratulations. It's you."*

In one corner of the platform stood the male half of the prom court. Darryl already had the Prom King crown on his head. He was flanked by three other boys from her class who wore blue sashes as the first, second and third princes.

The emcee, a deejay from a popular local radio station, came forward dramatically, brandishing an important-looking cream-colored envelope. He took out a card of the same color and began to read out the names of the third and second princesses.

Stella felt the hug of the last girl standing next to her seconds after she heard her name being called as Prom Queen. The president of the student council came forward and put a pink and gold sash over her shoulder, followed by the college dean who pinned a bejeweled tiara to her hair. She was hugged and kissed by a few more people before Darryl stood in front of her bearing a bouquet of white, yellow and pink flowers, mostly roses. Photographers surged forward and snapped pictures at an alarming, blinding rate.

She could hear the strains of David Pomeranz's song, 'King and Queen of Hearts,' coming over the speakers. This was the traditional Prom King and Queen dance.

The crowd applauded. The catcalls, whistles and whoops were deafening.

The skies responded, splitting open with a resounding, bright burst of lightning. Thunder followed, echoing through the sudden darkness that blanketed the entire pavilion.

"The power just went out," she heard the deejay say loudly. "Everyone please stay calm."

Someone grabbed her hand, pulling her to the left side of the stage. She thought at first it was Darryl, but she was certain he was on the opposite side of the stage, where moments before he stood under the spotlight with an obnoxious-looking bouquet in his hand and a silly grin on his face.

Stella found her voice, her hand instinctively going up to prevent the tiara on her head from falling. She could use it as a weapon, too, just in case.

"What the hell do you think you're doing?" she demanded.

"Hi, Stella." The voice came from the deepest shadows of stage left, the only sound she could hear clearly even with the rising din of people talking in the darkness.

She knew that voice.

"Trey?" she heard herself respond, in what sounded like a desperate whisper. Maybe she had completely lost it now.

Cellphones and lighters began coming to life on the pavilion floor, allowing her to see more clearly.

A single streak of light moved across the spot where she heard his voice coming from, falling on his profile for the briefest moment.

That was all she needed to see.

She unceremoniously pulled the errant tiara off her head and tossed it aside, then jumped off the stage and into his arms.

She landed on his chest, her fingers clutching the fabric of his shirt, her face burrowing into his neck, desperately taking in his familiar scent of pine and the sea.

Trey's hands were warm on her back. He was raining kisses on her hair and face. She knew the feeling of his lips on her skin.

"Let's get out of here," she heard him say.

Nothing in the world could stop her from going with him. She was not sure if he carried her, or she ran alongside him, but she found herself in a hut at the farthest end of the resort, cloaked by the night and the rain.

Before them, the surf crashed roughly against the shore. Their shelter of dried woven leaves made little consequence. They were both soaked to the skin.

It was only when he stood still before her, in the pale, thin light of the moon, was she finally convinced he was real. She reached out and touched his face, taking in all the planes and angles.

"I missed you so much," she said. "Whoever you are."

"It doesn't matter who I am. It never mattered to you."

He was right. It never did.

"What matters is that I love you." The words came out easily, as naturally as she breathed in the salty air and the heady scent of him. She touched the scar on his right cheek. She watched as he turned his head and started kissing her fingertips.

"You are so beautiful." His voice was equal parts passionate and tender, as was his gaze.

"So are you," she said, as she traced his lips and jawline.

"I came back to you," he said. "Do you know what that means?"

She put her arms around his torso, angling her ear so she could hear his heartbeat. "That you really love me? That you missed me, too?"

"It means I am yours, Stella. I have been yours the moment I saw you sitting in that intersection. I couldn't stop thinking about you. I tried to draw you. I never thought I could even touch you. You're an angel on earth I would die to protect."

She could feel the tears welling up behind her eyes, from the flood of emotion that overcame her.

But she didn't have time for tears now.

She only had time for him, because she belonged to him, too.

She reached up and put her hands on his shoulders, the same way she had all those months ago. She didn't have to pull him down. He lifted her off her feet to kiss her.

"I am yours, too," she said against his lips. "*Raphael. Trey.*"

She let the names roll off her tongue. There was nothing strange about them. They were both him.

Stella kissed him, then, before she finally called him what she had really wanted to, all these years.

"*My angel.*"

BOOK II
Heart Chained

Playlist

"Bring Me to Life"
Evanescence

"Everything"
Alanis Morissette

"One Last Breath"
Creed

"Into Your Arms"
Witt Lowry & Ava Max

"Here Without You"
3 Doors Down

"Gravity"
Sara Bareilles

"Stay"
Cueshe

One
THE RETURN

He was predictable, and she liked it that way. With Vincent Tugade, she always knew where she stood, what to expect. Everything about him was practically routine.

That morning, she immediately knew, the moment she saw a small box of cookies on her desk, that he was back. He had spent most of the past two months working offsite in Pampanga, in rounds of audits to wrap up the tax year. Although he wasn't the only auditor who had traveled there, she knew he was the only one who would remember to get her a gift, usually a sampling of the local delicacies.

Katrina David smiled and, delightedly, made her way across the building floor, from Human Resources to the side of the external auditors, which everyone in their firm called Assassins' Block.

Vincent's office was at a far corner, smaller than most but with an expansive view of Pasay City. The walls were almost bare except for a few framed certificates and photographs. It was always scented with the strong black coffee he drank all the time.

He was seated behind his two computer screens when she walked in. He looked up when he saw her. He jumped to his feet and swooped down on her for a hug.

"Welcome back, VAT," she said, putting her arms around him.

Years ago, when he first joined the firm, she had found his initials to be a little too fitting for his profession. As a result, she began using it. Then it stuck.

His familiar warmth was always comforting, as was the cool, subtle scent of his cologne.

"You look so brown. Eaten one too many plates of *sisig*?"

He laughed as he kissed her on the check. "Jealous much? It's good to be back. How have you been, Trina?"

"It's been busy around here," she said, giving him a peck in return. "I had no one to complain to these past few months, though. You missed a lot."

Vincent Alcon Tugade was the poster boy for yuppie Manila. He had classic Filipino looks, from his brown skin to his proud face with the hard planes, broad nose and dark eyes. He always dressed simply and elegantly, in light shirts and dark slacks, with hair neatly combed back. He appeared trustworthy and competent, without being obnoxious about any of it.

"I'm sure I did," he said. "With you around, I'll catch up in no time."

She sat on one of the chairs in front of his desk, one leg folded under her, and leaned forward. "How are you? Did anything exciting happen in Pampanga?"

"If you call spending fourteen hours a day with ledgers exciting, by all means, it was very exciting. I had the time of my life."

"You're no fun, Vince."

"You're welcome to all the fun, Trina." His smile at her was nothing if not indulgent, like a patient adult to a restless child. "I'll stick to my balance sheets. I don't think I've got energy for much else."

She frowned at him, exasperated but unsurprised. If he wasn't Vincent, she would have felt patronized. They were about the same age, but she had long since accepted that he behaved like a much older man. Her own father, who was into Airsoft and war games tournaments, was more fun than him.

She pouted at him. "Well, you'd better have enough energy to dance at my wedding, at least."

His hand froze over the computer mouse, just as one of his eyebrows shot up into his hairline. It took a second before he said anything.

"Abella asked?"

"He's going to." Trina saw he was about to say something more, but she stopped him by interrupting. "Soon. Maybe this weekend. We're having dinner on Saturday night. He's pulling out all the stops, VAT. Five-star hotel, the works."

She watched him lean back in his chair.

Broad-shouldered, well spoken, neat, and fairly easy to fit in the bill of tall, dark and handsome, he would have been very cute, she thought objectively, had he not been so boring.

Mature, she corrected herself, loyally. *He's just mature.*

"Well, in exchange for the cookies, I'm claiming first dibs on the happy news."

Trina stood up and rolled her eyes. She would have liked to stay if not for their department's Monday morning meeting.

"I've got to go for our team meeting. I never knew those cookies had a price, though."

"Miss David, you have worked for this firm your entire professional life." He switched to what she called his Presentation Mode, which he usually assumed in meetings with clients. It was the most deathly serious and, somehow, also one of the most comical voices she'd ever heard. "You should know by now that everything has a price."

Maybe he wasn't so boring, after all.

Two
THE SECRET

It was Saturday.

He picked up a dart from the coffee table in the middle of his apartment, aimed, and took the shot. The dart found its target, a small square of paper he had tacked to his reminders board.

Vincent walked up to the board and removed the dart. It had pierced right through the piece of desk calendar for that month, exactly where he had intended it to.

Today. *Saturday.*

He woke up that morning the same time he did every day, at five sharp. His apartment was close to Pasay City Sports Complex, so on most days he would go for a run. Today was no different.

After his run, he returned to his place and cooked oatmeal and eggs for breakfast. If he was not working weekends or on travel somewhere, he preferred staying in. If he had the chance, he would go out on Friday and Saturday nights.

Tonight, he definitely was going out. He needed to get out.

He had received the announcement the night before, at

eleven, by text message.

> R1: 100% Stock Engine & Chassis
> R2: Stock 4Stroke
> R3: Stock 4Stroke Automatic
> R4 Open to All Brands & Models
> Track: Legal confirm 8PM Sat 22/4
> Entry: TBC msg 9PM Sat 22/4

Vincent Tugade was a drag racer in the Manila underground circuit. His moniker, for many years now, was the King of Chains, from the insignia on the hood of his glistening black Dodge, paired with his signature leather clothing of the same color. His father had sketched this design for a race car back in the day; he had taken it upon himself to bring it to life.

He was into cars as far back as he could remember, spending long hours with his father at their garage during weekends, learning as much as he could about automobile design and engines.

Although his father had been a government tax official, his passion was customizing cars, which he had passed on to his son.

Vincent had been racing since he was eighteen, two years after his parents died from a freak traffic accident that involved a drunk driver ramming his pick-up truck into their own car. It was a bitter, ugly kind of irony.

He had uprooted himself and his little sister Veronica, ten years old at the time, from their province, and came to Metro Manila to live with one of their aunts, who taught at a Catholic private school. He had worked at the school as an errand boy at first, which led to the discovery of his near-prodigious understanding of numbers when he balanced the books of the school cafeteria and the uniform shop in less than a week.

Around the time, one of his jobs at his aunt's house was to look after her car, an ancient orange Toyota with manual transmission. He had been searching for a replacement for the stick shift at one of the shops in Makati when he overheard two men discussing an upcoming 'race.' That had piqued his curiosity in no time. Not long after, he had secretly souped up his aunt's ToyoPet and brought it for a run at an open race one night in late summer, just before he was due to start college.

By the time he graduated and got an Accountancy degree, he had garnered enough supporters and winnings to get his own car. An auditor's job allowed him more financial freedom to support his sister through university, buy a second car, and lease-to-own the condominium he now lived in.

Two years ago, his aunt had passed away quietly from a long-term illness. His little sister, after years of looking after their aunt, had decided to put her Nursing degree to good use and returned to their home province to take a high-profile clinical instructor job.

The glorious bachelor life allowed him to work as much as he liked with numbers during the day and race as much as he wanted at night. It was a simple delineation of the things he was good at.

He was on his second cup of coffee and was about to go downstairs to the parking basement to check his car for the night's race when his phone rang.

The name on the screen was the least expected of all. The presence of Katrina David was the only fluctuating value in the perfectly balanced books of his work and personal life.

He picked up the call.

"Hello, Trina." He tried to keep his voice as neutral as possible. "How are you?"

To his surprise, the response at the other end of the line was not the usual exuberant one he was familiar with. "Hi, Vince. I'm so sorry for bothering you. Did I call at a bad time?"

It was Trina, but she sounded so subdued it was like he was talking to an entirely different person.

"No, not at all. Everything okay?"

"You got a minute to talk? Please?"

No nicknames, no jokes, no comments on the absence of fun in his life. Maybe he had somehow wandered into a more depressing alternate reality after his early-morning run.

"Sure, of course. Anything for you." He took a seat on his couch. "What's up?"

"Nothing." There was a long, strained pause from her. "I mean, not nothing, but it's something I can't talk about with my parents or my friends."

"I'm all ears. What's this about?"

"James."

"Abella?"

The prick?

He wanted to tack on his opinion, but decided to keep his mouth shut.

The thought of James Abella, Trina's boyfriend, gave him the sudden urge to punch something. Vincent disliked him the same way he disliked racers who would rather spend money on a custom paint job than change their engine oil after a few races.

He had only met Abella three times at office functions over the past year or so but had long since formed the impression that the man was all flash, no substance. Perhaps a career in modeling did that to a person, but Vincent never generalized and only gave informed opinions. Since Trina was not a client, he kept whatever sentiments he had to himself.

"Has he done something? Are you okay?"

"Nothing like that. I'm fine."

He tried to be patient, thinking of the way he would usually talk to his little sister when she opened up about her relationships. "Okay, then, Trina. Just let me know if there's anything I can do."

Maybe, just maybe, run Abella over. She could pick which car I should

• •

use.

"Vince…what happens if I don't want to?"

"Don't want to what?"

"You know. The S-word."

He almost sputtered on his coffee. He slowly put his mug down on the table to avoid any further incident.

Damn. So much for your regular Saturday morning routine.

He held the phone away from his mouth as he took a deep breath before responding.

"I thought everything was done, dusted and double-ruled, all that. He was going to ask you to marry him, wasn't he?"

"He wants to take our relationship further, has wanted to for a while now. If he does ask me tonight to marry him and I say yes, he might want a…"

"Test drive?" He completed the statement and immediately regretted it.

"Yes." Deadpan and humorless, Trina had probably been replaced by an alien who happened to mimic her voice very well.

The silence on the line stretched for what seemed like hours.

There was only one response he could utter, the only one that mattered.

"What do you want to do?"

He heard a huge intake of breath, before she continued in a shaky voice. "I don't know. That's why I called you, to ask a man how he would feel if his fiancée refused to…you know."

This was dangerous ground. He would never speak for the prick.

"Has he asked you before?" He swallowed very hard before continuing. "Have you done it with him before?"

Fuck.

He could feel it. His face was going red. He was supposed to give advice on depreciation and inventory, not sex and relationships.

"No. Never. I tried, Vince. I can't…" Trina's voice trailed off.

He was tempted to ask why, but it wasn't the gentlemanly thing to do. If there was one thing he knew about women, it was to give them space.

As Trina went on, she sounded more and more anxious with each word. "He hasn't asked me straight out. But what he does when we're alone, it's enough to tell me what he really wants. I know I'm supposed to like it. He's my boyfriend, after all. But I can't seem to get myself to give in."

He listened to her breathing for several long moments before he spoke, as gently and as patiently as he could. "Then don't give in, if you don't want to."

"Wouldn't that frustrate him, or make him angry? Turn him off?"

Vincent knew about frustration very well, but this was not about him. "If he really loves you and wants to marry you, he should damn well be willing to wait until you're ready."

"Would you wait, Vince?" Her voice was quiet. "If you were in his place?"

"You know me better than that. I would never even consider putting you in a predicament like this. That's not love, Trina. Not even close."

Damn it to hell.

This wasn't supposed to be about him. Not in the fucking least.

"I never thought of it that way," she said. "When James first became my boyfriend, I was so happy. Everyone kept telling me how lucky I was."

Not everyone, he wanted to correct her.

"He is so handsome and dreamy, you know? He is a famous model and all that. I thought I have to keep him happy, to keep him."

"Are you happy now?" That seemed to be the last word he

could think of to describe her at the moment.

"To be honest, it's hard to be happy when your relationship is like a ticking time bomb. Lately, all I could think about is that it's only a matter of time before James asks. What if I can't give him what he wants? What if I make the wrong decision? What if he leaves me?"

It didn't sound like a healthy relationship. It sounded an awful lot like co-dependency.

"What if you think about what would make you happy, Trina?"

"Me? I don't know."

He couldn't blame her. Sometimes being in the safety of one's comfort zone mattered more than pursuing happiness. Sometimes the risk of getting out wasn't worth it, if it meant venturing into the unknown.

If it meant getting hurt.

"Once you figure it out, I get first dibs. I'll be here to listen. I might even splurge on some cookies. You know, those nasty sweet ones from Greenbelt you like so much."

He was rewarded by a small giggle. "Yeah, those."

"Think about what would make you happy, Trina, and make your decisions based on that. Not on what would make someone else happy, especially at your expense."

He hoped there was at least some clarity in her mind, or even a hint of a smile on her face.

"Thanks, VAT," she finally said. "You're the best, you know that?"

"Don't tell anyone, okay? My services are exclusive."

"To me?" He could hear the coyness, the humor, back in her voice. It was the best he could ask for, under the circumstances.

"Always have been."

"See you Monday, Vince. I'm really sorry if I bothered you on your weekend."

"It's okay. You can bother me anytime."

Trina thanked him again and hung up.

He stood up, plugged the phone into its charger, and sat back down on the couch. He picked up his mug for a sip. The coffee was now cold and flat, almost bitter.

He felt just as cold and flat as he thought of Abella, with her.

Trina.

He first met her six years ago, when she did his pre-interview at the firm. She was the most breathtaking woman he had ever laid eyes on, an opinion the years had not changed. She had smooth caramel skin, an hourglass figure, and long wavy hair a deep shade of mahogany. Her face had a sincere warmth he could just stare at and drink in for hours.

His first impression was that she was the human equivalent of the Energizer bunny, someone who kept going and going and barely stopped talking while at it.

Instead of finding her lively manner annoying, he found himself warming up, to the point of allowing her to christen him with a new nickname. It was little wonder she was the one usually assigned to potential hires or new employees.

It was a wonder, however, how they became friends. The first thing he could think of was how she could so easily get him to open up, or at least talk. Other people at the firm, even his fellow auditors, gave him space to work and move around the office without much need for social interaction. He had a reputation for no-frills efficiency, and he had to admit it commanded respect.

Trina did not give him the wide berth others did. She simply found her way into his life and settled in it, the same way she would barge into his office any time she wanted and sit in weird positions on the chairs facing his desk. Their friendship had lasted the better part of the past five years, to the point that his sister thought she was his girlfriend when Trina showed up at their aunt's funeral.

Now, he pondered the advice he had given her.

Think about what would make you happy.

Was he a hypocrite to give a confused woman this kind of advice, when he couldn't even apply it to his own life?

Then again, he wasn't the one in a relationship, not the one who faced the risk of a broken heart.

Or was he?

He knew from the moment Trina had started talking about things getting serious with Abella that his own heart was on the line. It was only a matter of time before it got ripped into shreds. He predicted it would either be at the sight of a ring on her finger or of the very woman herself in a wedding dress.

He was prepared for it, as long as she didn't know. He could face it, the same way he had faced life when it came to her.

Held back by chains of his own making.

Three
THE RAIN

*D*one, *dusted and double ruled.*

Vincent's words echoed in her mind as she lifted her chin and walked straight into the drizzling Manila night, ignoring the politely disguised yet obviously curious stares of the doorman and security guard stationed at the hotel's front entrance.

More like fully depreciated and written off.

She was a fool to think there would be at least some sort of compromise, that James would give her room to think about what she really wanted.

Instead, he had wined and dined her, then went in for the kill.

It shouldn't have surprised her.

The rain was the first one that month, adding insult to her already dreary state of affairs. The typhoon season was still months away, but, hell, anything goes.

Life seemed to be trying to throw as much crap as it could at her, all at the same time.

The hotel was located in the Bay Area, close to the

metropolitan but posh and exclusive enough to merit its high profile and ludicrously expensive status.

There should be a few taxis around, in theory, but everyone drove their shiny, showy cars to and from this place, as far as she could see.

She was the only one walking.

She could wait inside for a taxi, but she had more pride than that. No way in hell was she staying.

Trina clutched her leather handbag tightly, debating whether or not to use it as some kind of umbrella, finally dismissing the idea as pointless.

Her little black dress and matching suede shoes had already gone to waste. She wished she had not splurged as much during her shopping trip that afternoon, in an effort to keep her mind off the conversation with Vincent and the inevitable with James.

The downpour had increased in intensity by the time she reached the main gates of the hotel. Half-blinded by rain water, she continued to plod onwards.

"I met someone else, Trina."

Those five words tolled at the back of her head like some kind of death knell.

James had gone on and on with his explanation. Perhaps he'd thought it would make her feel better, if there was a clear reason for their break-up.

"I thought you loved me, but I never felt it. She made me feel loved, in ways more than words could ever explain."

Feel it, my ass, she thought bitterly.

"I tried to make our relationship work but nothing ever seemed to get through to you. I hope you'll understand where I'm coming from. I've fallen in love with her."

The funny part was that she understood very clearly, maybe a little too well for her own good.

The moment her now-ex-boyfriend had finished his

confession, she had stood up, with as much dignity as she could muster, and made the most regal exit she could from the restaurant.

She took pride in two things: First, she'd kept her head held high; second, she'd never cried.

She had no desire to cry. If anything, she could almost describe her feelings, after the initial hurtful blow of rejection to her ego, as a combination of relief and lightness, as if she'd just been unburdened of something ridiculously heavy.

"Think about what would make you happy, Trina."

She would give anything right now, if she could just talk to Vincent.

Anything to hear his voice, always a source of comfort and reason.

As soon as she got home, she'd try and give him a call…

A sudden, deafening screech cut through the fog of her thoughts.

She momentarily forgot her troubles as she, dazed and confused, faced the direction of the high-pitched sound.

A black car, with prism-like headlights, had stopped a few feet away from her. She stared as the car's wipers moved furiously, rhythmically, across the windshield.

She had not seen any cars coming her way. There was no one else outside, no one else on the road. Not in this weather.

She was meant to be on her own tonight, wasn't she? Chained to her own thoughts and, even more so, her regrets.

But it wasn't meant to be.

Four
THE RACE

TRINA

It was time.

Even after all these years, anticipation gripped him at the thought of a race.

The feeling was familiar: the slight acceleration of his heartbeat, the clammy sensation in his palms, the tightness in his stomach. Soon enough, nerves would give way to focus; and focus would eventually explode into all-consuming adrenaline once the flag came down.

In the dimly lit garage of his apartment building, the sleek form of his car, whom he'd named *Eskeleto*, stood before him, ready to carry him into yet another race.

He inspected every inch of the vehicle, ensuring its peak performance. He let his hands run over the smooth curves of the car, grounding himself in the present, as far as he possibly could from thoughts that threatened to invade his impeccably crafted sense of concentration.

Right now, he hated the accuracy and precision of his memory. Because of it, there were images of Trina floating at the fringes of his mind, clawing at the walls he had so carefully built to keep his emotions in check.

"Let's do this, old friend," he said to *Eskeleto*.

Just like the well-worn leather jacket he had on, the car's hood bore his insignia of a skull encircled by a chain and an antique pocket watch.

It was as fearsome a symbol as it was poetic; a juxtaposition of life, death, and the confines of mortality.

Time.

What he wouldn't give to have more time with Trina, before she went on with her life and rode off into the sunset with her male model.

He sighed.

He really was fucked.

He had no choice now but to deal with it head on, all cylinders firing.

He had to deal with the thought of losing Trina.

As the King of Chains of the Manila drag race circuit, he had one glaring solution to his current predicament: *Drive.*

Vincent slipped behind the wheel and switched the ignition, his hands settling comfortably on the steering wheel.

Next to *Eskeleto* stood his other car, the dark grey Toyota sedan he used to drive to work and other more everyday places. He'd named the car *T-Baby.*

Thinking about himself doing something so juvenile and lovesick was almost painful.

At least, *T-Baby* was there to stay.

As *Eskeleto* roared to life beneath him, he allowed the sound to drown out all else. With one last glance at his other car, as if bidding farewell to a part of him that still clung to the possibility of going in another direction, towards a different destination, he revved the engine and sped off into the night.

The city lights blurred together as he drove through the

streets. He knew each race demanded every ounce of skill, focus and determination he could muster. He couldn't afford to give in to sentimentality or distractions.

He made it to the venue with time to spare. Situated next to Manila Bay, the track was abuzz with the frenetic energy of the underground scene, where the salty breeze coming in from the sea mingled with the scents of rubber and gasoline. The sounds of engines revving and people shouting greetings and good-natured taunts to each other were comforting to his ears, a welcome diversion from his inner turmoil.

He parked in his designated spot near the track, the area marked by a replica of his skull symbol using temporary neon paint. He took a deep breath and stepped out of the car to check in with the organizers of the evening's race.

"King of Chains!" a voice called out.

A group of younger racers, clustered along with their brightly colored sports cars, looked at him with awe and reverence.

"H-hey, boss," one of them stammered, extending a trembling hand. "Good luck tonight!"

"Thanks," Vincent replied, forcing a smile for their benefit. "Good luck to all of you. Let's have a good race tonight."

As he shook hands with well-wishers, he allowed himself to slip into his track persona: someone confident, untouchable, and utterly devoted to the thrill of the race.

"Vincent! Over here!" a chorus of female voices beckoned him from a nearby cluster of cars.

He turned to see a gaggle of beautiful women, some draped over sleek hoods and others leaning against gleaming fenders. A few cast sultry glances his way.

"Looking good tonight, Vincent," purred one woman whose perfectly made-up face he'd seen at almost every race for the past few years.

Her name was Alena; she drove a custom red Volvo that he was quite sure was also bulletproof.

"How about we celebrate your victory together later?" Her voice was heavily laced with suggestive promise.

"Sorry, beautiful, not tonight," he replied with a polite smile. "Got to travel for work tomorrow."

Though his reputation on the track often attracted such propositions, tonight his heart and mind were too preoccupied to entertain even the fleeting distractions of flirtation and casual sex.

"Always so focused," another woman teased, boldly stepping closer to ruffle his hair. It was Florence, an oil tycoon's daughter, who drove an import Lamborghini that probably cost more than a lifetime's worth of his salary. "That's what makes you the best."

"I'll make it up to you next time, ladies," he promised with a grin, though the words felt hollow to his ears.

As he turned away from the women and eventually found his way to the organizers, the clamor of the race track seemed to amplify within his head.

He *needed* tonight's race, more than he'd ever needed any other race before.

Trina.

The name echoed through this head, almost forming on his lips like a prayer for salvation.

His prayer was answered not too long after, when he found himself flanked by two other cars on each side at the starting line.

His opponents were mere shadows in his peripheral vision, their presence barely registering as his hands settled on the wheel with the familiarity of a swordsman with his trusty katana.

"Are you ready?" came a woman's voice through a megaphone. "It's time for the final race!"

That night's honorary marshal was a beauty queen from a neighboring country. She was unbelievably attractive in person, with a glistening black bob, legs that went on for days, and a tiny waist cinched in by the matching belt of her red dress.

She held up a racing flag in the air, her movement punctuated by excited cheers and roars of the crowd.

"GO!"

In an instant, the world around him melted away, fading into streaks of color as his car shot forward like a bullet from a gun. Adrenaline surged through his veins as he expertly navigated the twists and turns of the track.

As he raced towards the finish line, the cheers of the crowd reverberated in his ears, but none quite reached him.

He knew what was missing, but he also knew he had to keep himself in check long enough to finish what he'd started. The final stretch lay before him, a straight path to victory.

And, just like that, it was over.

Vincent and *Eskeleto* crossed the finish line, the other racers and their cars still dozens of meters behind.

The moment he stepped out of the car, he was surrounded by a boisterous crowd. He lost count of the handshakes, hugs, and kisses he was given, but he took it all in stride.

Somehow, tonight, he didn't feel the usual rush of victory. The end of the race, albeit one he'd won, felt like signing off the financial statements of a client at the end of a lengthy audit.

It was a job he did well, a job he'd completed meticulously and painstakingly. No more, no less.

"Nice win, King of Chains," one of his opponents called out, clapping him on the shoulder.

"Thanks, Phil," he replied, forcing a smile.

As the last remnants of the crowd dispersed into after-parties and the track finally fell silent, Vincent climbed back into his car.

Just as he started the drive back to his apartment, opting for a shortcut through the Bay Area, it began to rain.

The streets of late-night Manila stretched out before him like a labyrinth, but he realized there was no escaping the thoughts that haunted him, no matter where he went.

He could drive fast, drive away, or even drive endlessly. These were all tempting options, but he knew, in the end, escape was impossible.

Vincent knew he could never outrun his thoughts of her, tightly chained to his memories and his heart.

He didn't even get that far when he saw her in the middle of the rain-slicked road. Shock mingling with disbelief, he dimly heard the tires screech as he hit the brakes.

Heart pounding, he stared at the drenched figure standing outside his car, illuminated by *Eskeleto*'s headlights.

It's not a mirage, he thought, his head spinning.

He would recognize the real Trina anywhere.

Was it a sign, or some kind of twisted joke?

There was only one way to find out.

He pushed the car door open and stepped out into the downpour.

Five
THE STRANGER

A man, dressed all in the same color as the dark vehicle before her, stepped out of the car.

His clothing was shiny, like leather. With his hair styled into spikes, he looked like a sleek nocturnal animal, or maybe the lead singer of a rock band.

"Trina? What the fuck are you doing here?"

The voice was very familiar, but the sight wasn't. The rain and the headlights danced around her like strobes in a disco, making her dizzy.

She had to make sense of this.

So she uttered his name, in both uncertainty and unabashed curiosity.

"Vincent?"

The man who sounded but barely looked like Vincent Tugade sloshed his way to her side, his eyes glittering even in the cover of night.

"Have you lost your mind, Trina? You shouldn't be out on the road like this."

"Vincent?" she repeated the name, not quite sure if she wanted to be right or wrong. "What are you doing here? Why do you look like that?"

"We have to get you off the streets." He held out a hand to her. "Come on."

She could only stare at him. The dinner, the near-accident, now this man. It was too much.

"Get in the car, Trina, please."

She backed away. She didn't have the energy to put up with more surprises tonight. "Just go, okay? Leave me alone."

"What are you doing?" He stepped closer and took hold of her arm. "I'm taking you home, okay? Please get in the car and we can talk about it."

He gave her that familiar indulgent smile, none too sincerely this time. She recognized him like this, vaguely.

"I don't think—"

Before she could continue, he had his hand on the small of her back and was guiding her to the car. Too weary to put up a fight, she allowed herself to be pushed, albeit gently, into the front seat.

He silently got into the driver's side. In the dim light, she could see his lips set in a firm line. He took off his jacket and gave it to her. He was dressed in a black sleeveless shirt underneath.

"Stay warm. I'll turn off the air conditioner."

"Thanks," she heard herself say.

"You're welcome."

He reached for the dashboard and started adjusting buttons and switches. His arms had well-defined muscles and an assortment of tattoos going all the way down to his forearms.

To stop herself from staring at him so rudely, Trina gave the jacket a shake and put it around her shoulders. She could feel her new dress soak water into the car seat. She buckled up when she saw him do the same. She clutched her bag and the seatbelt close to her as she looked out of the window at the rainy night.

The car hummed to life and started to cruise forward.

"Vince, I…" It took a while before she could work up the energy and courage to look at the almost-stranger next to her, much less talk to him.

"I'm sorry," she completed lamely, clenching her hands, feeling them shake with the residual cold.

He was quiet for several seconds. "For what?"

"For all the trouble. One thing after another went downhill. Before I knew it, I was out of there like my ass was on fire."

He shook his head, but kept his eyes trained on the road. "In a way, it's a good thing I was the one you ran into. The car's brakes hold up pretty well even when they're wet."

The thought of brakes was enough to make her feel even colder. Had it been another car, or another driver, she wasn't quite sure where she would be now.

In hindsight, she should have stayed inside the hotel and waited for a taxi, or got James to drop her home, not wandered out into the rain like some tragic heroine in a cheap romance novel. The only real tragedy of the entire evening was the sorry shape of her pricey new dress and its matching shoes.

"Still, this entire drama is my fault," she admitted.

"Drama?"

"The walk-out, the emoting in the rain, the getting nearly ran over part. I guess I was too proud to put up with any more bullshit."

"I see." Vincent held on to the steering wheel with one hand, his other hand going up to rub out droplets of water stuck to his spiky hair. "I'm sure that wasn't how you had the night planned out, was it?"

"Well, no." She gave her eyes a little rub, still unable to reconcile the fact that this tattooed, leather-clad man was the Vincent she had known all these years. She didn't even know he had arms like that.

For the first time, she noted that this wasn't his Toyota sedan, but something else entirely.

The black car had metal panels on the sides, a convex roof and a windshield lined with what looked like steel reinforcements. The seats were wrapped in dark leather that matched his clothes. All over the interior, there were stickers and buttons with death motifs, such as skulls, chains and spikes. The buttons and gauges on the dashboard before her looked like the control panel of a mad scientist.

His voice was calm and measured as he spoke. "If I had known you were going to be at the hotel, I would have picked you up. You should have called me."

"I dragged you through the pathetic story of my relationship this morning. I could never do that to you twice. Besides, I never thought you would be here, at this time. Like that." She gestured to all of him in general.

"Like what?" He glanced at her, tilting his head curiously.

"Like, different. Dangerous. You know, someone capable of running James over."

To her surprise, he smiled. "Whoever said I wasn't? All you have to do is ask."

She sighed. "That sounds very tempting right now."

His next words were so serious it was hard to discern whether or not he really meant them. "If you really want to do a number on Abella, we can turn back and get him. The track near the bay will be closed by now, but I'm sure I could get us in. I've raced there since they started building it, right after the mall opened."

Race.

VAT was a racer. Suddenly, the car, the clothes and the skulls all made sense.

"Thanks for the generous and potentially criminal offer, but I'll pass." She could feel the beginnings of a small smile on her lips.

They didn't talk for a while as he deftly wove the car through the Saturday night traffic of the city, taking shortcuts through tiny side streets. By the time they were out of the Bay Area, she felt calm enough to loosen her grip on her bag and the seatbelt and settle more comfortably in the front seat.

"You still live at the tower?"

"Yes. I'm surprised you remember."

He shrugged. "We should be there soon. I know a shortcut near the hospital. That should keep us away from most of the late night traffic."

"You're the best, VAT," she said, echoing her sentiments from earlier that day. "Thanks for putting up with my crap."

He didn't answer, but a little while later she felt his hand on her shoulder.

"It's not crap. I'm very sorry this happened." He gave a gentle squeeze before letting go. "You deserve to be happy."

She tugged at his jacket, pulling it more snugly around her. She never knew leather could feel so soft.

"At least James had the guts to call it off himself. I suppose he needed something I couldn't give. We both wanted different things. I stressed all about it for nothing."

Vincent shook his head. "Not nothing. I'm sure whatever you two had, it meant more to you than it did to him."

Trina looked out the window again. She could barely see a thing, except for torrents of water, thick mist, and flickering lights.

It was a fitting metaphor for what she had with James. What she thought she had with him. She never really saw what it was, just blurry lines and splashes of color. Everything she made out of it was her own interpretation, not the truth.

Her newly-ended relationship was a joke, if not a failure, from the very start. Marrying her was something James had never even remotely considered. She knew that now.

"James told me he met someone else while on a job in Bali months back. It doesn't take a genius to figure out he got what he wanted from her. Apparently they kept in touch after that."

The memory of her ex's confession was still fresh in her mind, spilling out easily. Trina couldn't even remember the other girl's name. "James said she was far less…I don't know, frigid than I am, I suppose. The exact words he used were 'cold' and 'walled off.'"

"Sounds like he thinks you're some kind of high security vault. One he doesn't have the access code to, the poor bastard."

"I never thought you'd ever feel sorry for him." She gave him a sidelong glance. "You hate his guts."

"Am I that obvious?"

"Kind of, especially as you offered to run him over if I wanted you to."

"That prick doesn't know what he's missing out on," he declared solemnly, in a tone that begged no argument.

Minutes later, they pulled up in front of a high-rise condominium complex. He parked in an open spot on the sidewalk, got out of the car, and opened the passenger door for her.

She shakily stepped out, her wet shoes digging into her skin as she walked carefully on the rain-drenched pavement. Her dress had dried partially, but it still clung to her body like a second skin. To her surprise, she felt self-conscious under the bright fluorescent lights of the building's main entrance as he followed her to the foyer.

"Thank you, Vince." She pulled his jacket off her shoulders and handed it back to him. "For everything."

"You're welcome." He reached out and took the jacket back. "Will you be okay? Can I get you anything, from the pharmacy or somewhere?"

"No, I'm fine. Thanks for the offer." No matter how he dressed, he was always reliable.

Tonight, he just appeared a little more exciting than usual.

It occurred to her how different it had felt to look at her ex-boyfriend's mestizo, camera-ready face, compared to the darker, harder countenance of the man before her.

With Vincent, she had always been at ease. She never had to second-guess herself or question her own actions and decisions.

His words in the car rattled around the back of her mind.

That prick doesn't know what he's missing out on.

What if she asked herself that question?

What am I missing out on?

He was looking straight back at her. She had no idea what was in his head. She never really had. She'd always expected him, by default, to come through, listen, accept, and give – cookies, advice, time, his presence. He even came through for her at this time, without her asking, without him knowing, by sheer chance of fate.

Why did he?

Trina didn't know if she felt guilty, confused or overwhelmed. Perhaps all three. Seeing Vincent in a different light, in the rainy cold of reality, was unnerving.

She needed to put this entire weekend behind her, as soon as possible.

He stepped closer and wrapped one arm around her shoulders. He gave her a quick peck on the cheek; it felt familiar, yet, in her waterlogged state, she felt a little breathless at the contact. She could feel blood rushing to her head.

"Rest up, Trina," he said as he pulled away. "Call me tomorrow if you need anything, okay?"

She didn't let him pull away completely. Instead, she put her hands on his tattooed forearms. Still halfway in his embrace, she could see that his eyes were almost silver in color, not the greyish-brown she thought they were.

"Would you like to come up for some coffee?" Her own

voice sounded higher-pitched, even shrill, to her own ears. She had no idea where it came from, but it was all her.

He hesitated. He was still predictable enough, but she had always liked that about him. She knew his answer before he said it, but she didn't quite anticipate the tension she felt emanating from his body.

"Sure."

<h1 style="text-align:center">Six
THE TURN</h1>

What the fuck are you doing, Tugade?

Vincent mentally confronted himself as he followed her off the elevator. They had reached the seventh floor of her apartment building.

"My place is this way." Trina was a few steps ahead. He could see she was limping a little and dragging her feet. He thought of helping her, but the idea of touching her again didn't sound very smart at the moment.

He shouldn't have touched her like he had downstairs. They had always hugged and kissed each other chastely, but, tonight, it felt very different. For starters, she kept giving him wide-eyed looks, from all directions, as if she was seeing him for the first time.

Vince knew those kinds of looks. He had given her those before, many times over, when he was certain she couldn't see him. He had never stopped, not since he first saw her when she came out to the firm's lobby for his pre-interview.

He knew his feelings for her very well, had grappled with

and successfully kept them buried under a platonic veneer. Trina, on the other, had no idea. If she did, she would probably be out of his life like her 'ass was on fire.'

It was a risk he could not take. He had too much to lose. Her friendship, her trust, and, above all, *her.*

Katrina David was someone he could never afford to lose.

With her freshly single from a break-up, this was the worst possible time to even consider that he had a chance. He would rather have himself run over on the track by the other racers.

Trina stopped at a unit numbered 704. "Home sweet home. Can you help me, Vince?"

He had to snap himself out of any delusional episode he had going. She was holding out her keys.

"The gold one, please."

He took the bunch rather abruptly from her grasp and moved closer to the door. As he bent over to unlock it, he felt Trina wrap her arms around his left arm as she leaned against him. Up close, he could see her wet dress hugging every curve of her body. Her cleavage was practically next to his face as she shifted her weight from foot to foot.

"I'm so tired, Vince," she said. "I think I spent next month's salary shopping this afternoon for an outfit that I completely ruined."

Ruined? That was the last thing on his mind, looking at her in the little black dress.

He averted his eyes and thanked all existing higher powers when he heard the lock give way. He was too close for comfort. He would have that coffee and get himself the fuck home.

She did not let him go as they went in, clinging to his arm as she hobbled into the apartment and pointed out the light switches. He gave in to his earlier gentlemanly inclination and led her to the white couch in the middle of her living room. She heaved herself gratefully onto the seat and took off her shoes.

"Major ouch." She shook her head and made clucking

sounds as she started flexing her toes and rotating her ankles.

He took the opportunity to step away from her. He could leave. She was fine. He had made sure of that.

"I think I'll call it a night," he said. "I'd better go."

True to form, Trina hopped back to her bare feet. "What are you talking about? Sit down. Let me get you that coffee. It's premium roasted Arabica. I'll even give you the rest of the beans, too."

He swallowed hard and seated himself hesitantly on the couch, next to the spot she had just vacated. He tossed his jacket to a nearby plastic chair. "I'm sorry about the wet clothes."

"I did the same thing to your car. Call it even between us."

He watched her disappear behind a curtained doorway. He looked around. The place was neat and orderly; the colors were a mishmash of white, brown, orange and yellow. Even on a rainy night, the place looked bright and alive.

Minutes later, he saw her head poke through the curtains. "Vince? Come join me in the kitchen. I put on some croissants, too."

"That would be great." He stood up and followed her into the next room. It was fairly compact, cozy, outfitted with sunny yellow tiles. Next to a small glass window overlooking the city, there was a wooden table with matching seats for three.

She gestured for him to sit on one of the chairs. She was quiet as she poured them both coffee. She placed a plate full of croissants between them and sat from across him.

"Thanks for looking out for me tonight. Goodness knows I have no business troubling you for anything. I honestly thought this morning was the end of it."

He took a sip of the coffee. It was strong and scalding hot. "Is that how you think of yourself, Trina? Trouble?"

He watched her take a sip of coffee, twitching a little uncomfortably in her damp dress as she thought about his question. He wondered if it would be appropriate if he suggested she change clothes, more for his state of mind than her own health and comfort.

"It seems I could never give anyone what they want from me," she declared thoughtfully. "I don't know if that's trouble or not."

"It's called making your choices, I believe. Definitely not trouble."

Trina shrugged. "Is it? James thinks I'm a cold bitch. My friends think I'm so flighty I couldn't even commit to their vacation plans. My own family thinks I'm all talk and no substance, that's why I haven't been promoted to HR Manager."

The rapid-fire honesty in her declaration was a heart-rending surprise. He was sorely tempted to close the distance between them and take her into his arms.

Instead, he took another sip of coffee. "Do you agree with any of them?"

She shook her head. "I love my job and I like people. I actually enjoy my work. If I were manager, I would have to spend the whole damn day writing reports, signing stupid forms, and talking to higher management. As for trips, I don't really want to go on a lot of them because traveling's so expensive and I want to pay off this unit as soon as possible."

Her down-to-earth practicality was something he admired immensely. "Can't argue with the numbers on that one."

"I know, right?" Her shoulders heaved in a sigh. "And James…well, tonight pretty much sums it all up. For the record, he broke it off, but I was the one who walked out first."

"There you go. You've made your choices. If people don't appreciate that, it's their problem, not yours."

She smiled at him for what seemed the first time that evening. "I think you're right."

"You should start thinking about what you want, rather than what other people want and expect from you. As I said, you deserve to be happy. Do what makes you happy."

If only he could do the same thing. If only he had the balls to follow his own advice.

Her smile brightened a little more. "This makes me happy. Having you here."

It felt as if she had stabbed him, front and center. To disguise the tightness in his chest, he affected a grin and lifted his coffee mug in a toast. "To your happiness, Trina."

She leaned forward, wrapping her hands around her mug. Her eyes narrowed, focusing on him like laser beams, as if she was trying to read his thoughts.

"Why do you do this, Vince?"

"Do what?"

"This. You look after me. Without asking for anything in return."

He swallowed the bite of croissant in his mouth. "We're friends. That's what friends do."

"I don't really know anything about you, do I? I mean, you've never even told me you had a car like that, or you race...I don't even know if you have a girl waiting for you somewhere and, somehow, tonight her man's babysitting me instead. That kind of thing."

He had to smile at her words. She always gave him more credit than he deserved, especially with women. "You know there is no girl. There's no one. As for racing, it's something you don't exactly advertise when you work in a Big Four firm."

"Will you take me to a race next time?"

"I'll take you, just promise you won't tell anyone in the office. With that dress, you'll fit right in."

"This outfit has not been a total waste, then."

"No, not at all." After a quick glance at his watch, he got to his feet. All that talk about his personal life and the absence of romance from it was making him uncomfortable. She would prod and pry all the time, but when she suggested becoming part of it, even in a race, it made him feel exposed, vulnerable.

"It's late, Trina. I'd better go."

She nodded and got up, too, following him back to her colorful living room. She handed over his jacket and a paper bag. "The coffee, as promised. If you do decide to bring it to work on Monday, save some for me."

"Not a chance," he said, grinning down at her.

Instead of responding by whacking him on the arm or giving one of her usual silly faces, Trina stared at him with wide, almost doe-like, eyes. She put her arms around his shoulders and invaded what little personal space there was left between them, never taking her gaze off him.

"Trina?" he asked, hesitantly, trapped but not exactly unwilling. "What are you doing?"

"What makes me happy."

With her fingers in his hair, she brought his head down for a kiss.

Seven
THE HEART

She heard his sharp intake of breath, felt a sudden tautness take over his body. Something fell to the floor, crunching under their feet. The world around them began to spin as she pushed her body against his.

This was something she had never wanted to do with James.

With Vincent, it was the exact opposite. The moment he gave her that big smile, there was nothing more she wanted in the world than to get all that leather off him and have him for herself

She didn't want him to go.

The desire she felt was as clear as the sky on a bright, sunny day. There was neither confusion nor uncertainty. There was only the feeling she was exactly where she was meant to be, with the person she was meant to be with.

His arms, wonderfully warm through her damp clothes, went around her as he started to kiss her back, slowly at first, then with more urgency. He tasted of coffee and rain, of salt and a hint of sugar. She couldn't get enough of it.

In that moment, she realized what she had known, in the deepest and darkest corner of her heart, all along.

It has always been Vincent Tugade.

Kissing alone wouldn't satisfy her. She had never been more certain of something, ever. Her hands took a life of their own, moving beneath his shirt, until she could feel the hardness of his torso under her fingertips.

He didn't keep idle. He nipped at her earlobes and neck as he began to push the straps of the black dress off her shoulders, baring a wider path for his lips to trace.

She moaned when his mouth found its way to her collarbone. She dug her fingers into his back as he devoured the sensitive skin of her throat and chest.

She found her voice and, for what seemed like the very first time, the words to tell him what she truly wanted.

"Please don't go. Don't leave me tonight."

As if wrenched from a dream, he stopped, his hands still on her back, in her hair.

"Trina…" he breathed, his eyes clouding. "I'm sorry."

Her heart was still pounding so loudly in her ears, she could barely hear him. She gripped his shoulders tightly as she fought to catch her breath.

"Sorry? Sorry for what?" She dared herself to look into his eyes.

His silvery gaze seared its way into her soul. She had to look away. She knew she would burn to a bittersweet death if she looked any longer.

"I can't do this, Trina." His voice was subdued, almost melancholic.

"Do what?" Her own response was just as muted.

"I care about you too much to do this now. You deserve so much better than this."

"Vince, please…" She didn't know what she was asking for.

She only knew, at that moment, that she didn't just want him.

She needed him.

He untangled his arms from around her body, but he stayed close enough to cup her face in his hands. "This isn't me rejecting you or us. It's about respecting your feelings and our friendship."

She leaned into his touch. He had to know. Just as she had to go through tonight to find out the truth for herself.

"There's something I need to tell you," she said determinedly, trying to ignore the shakiness and fear in her voice.

He reached for her hand and gave it a reassuring squeeze. "What is it?"

She took a deep breath. "It has always been you."

The words came out in a rush, so she chased after what little bravado she had left. "I never knew how to say it before, because you seemed so unreachable, so... grown-up and perfect."

Vincent didn't say anything, but he stared at her, unblinking, seemingly stunned by the weight of her words.

"Every time I was with someone else, I couldn't help but compare them to you," she continued. "That's why I could never truly be with anyone else—because they would always fall short of what I felt for you. They could never measure up to you, VAT. No one could."

When he finally moved, his reaction was the last thing she expected. He focused on helping her straighten her clothes, his fingers gentle as he smoothed out the creases from her dress like an attentive parent.

When he was done, he pulled her back into his arms for a gentle hug and pressed a soft kiss to her forehead. "Good night, Trina. I'll see you Monday."

Just as he took a step back, her anger flared.

"Good night? That's all you have to say?" She invaded his personal space once more, glaring at him, her raw vulnerability quickly replaced by indignation. "After all we've been through, that's all you've got to say? I don't think you've ever really cared for me, Tugade. All these years, and you never once showed me how much I meant to you!"

In sharp contrast to her biting tone, his response was soft. "That's not true, Trina."

"Isn't it? If you really cared, you would have been smart enough to figure out my feelings for you by now. You would have seen through all my smiles and my teasing, and you would have recognized that it was my love I was trying to hide from you."

"Trina, I..." The words seemed caught in his throat. His face was deathly pale.

He looked a bit like the skull on his jacket, she thought bitterly, stepping away from him and averting her eyes, unable to put up with all the uncertainty surrounding them like a poisonous fog.

"Trina," he began again, more slowly and quietly this time. "I don't just care for you. I love you."

His words landed like a physical blow.

Their meaning was so strong, she was almost thrown backwards onto the floor. Instead, she planted her feet firmly into her damp carpet, stubbornly staring at the wall before her.

Stubbornly refusing to accept what she had just heard.

Vincent didn't stop there. "Maybe that's why you couldn't see it. Caring is something clear, something easily understood. But love..." His voice trailed off, as if he was searching for the right words. "Love is so much more. It's complicated and messy and just plain fucked up. I could never figure out how to show you how I really felt. There's no formula on how to do it."

To her surprise, she felt tears well up in her eyes, taking down the last few pieces that remained of her battered pride. She prayed fervently he couldn't see them—or the pathetic look on her face.

There was a weighted pause before she heard him speak again. "Goodbye, Trina."

She heard a faint rustle as he picked up his jacket from the floor. After a few light footsteps and the creaking of her front door, he was gone.

When she finally had the strength to look, she saw that he'd left the bag of coffee beans behind.

It hurt to move from her spot in the middle of the living room. It was even more excruciating for her to walk to the door and lock it.

She did the only thing she could to ease the pain.

She sat on the couch and gave her tears permission to fall.

Eight
THE CHAINS

He felt numb.

He was grateful he could still move after everything that happened in Trina's apartment. His entire body felt frozen and unwilling as he made his way back down the hall and took the elevator. He felt as if he'd run a marathon and then took a beating after.

Vincent climbed into his car and drove away from her building. Through the veil of the ongoing downpour, the streets were nearly empty in the late hour. The deafening roar of his thoughts seemed even more pronounced against the stillness of the world around him.

Why did he leave?

Trina had told him she didn't want him to go. He replayed her words in his mind over and over, each repetition making him question his decision more and more.

"It has always been you."

Wasn't he chained to her all these years? He had always felt that invisible bond connecting them, drawing him closer to her even when he tried to pull away.

"Fuck it all," he muttered under his breath, his hands shaking as he held the steering wheel as tightly as he could, fearing his self-control would slip away at any moment.

Why had he run away now, when she needed him most? Was it fear that held him back? Fear of admitting to himself and to her how much she really meant to him?

He breathed out slowly, trying to calm his racing heartbeat that mirrored the engine's purr.

"Trina," he whispered into the darkness, as if saying her name might bring him a measure of clarity. "I'm sorry, baby. I love you."

As soon as the words left his mouth, he realized that he was making a grave mistake. That the love he had kept bottled up for so long would remain unacknowledged if he didn't turn back.

He couldn't run away now.

He could never run away, in the first place, even if he tried.

Katrina David would always pull at his chains with a single glance, a soft smile, a teasing word; and he would be back right by her side, where he knew he'd always belonged.

Eskeleto's tires screeched on the pavement as he made an abrupt U-turn, his decision made. The streets whirred past him like a kaleidoscope, but all he could focus on was the burning resolve within him.

He accelerated, pushing his car to its limits, just as he would on the track.

But, this time, it was different.

It was a race he didn't want to win. It was a race he desperately wanted to finish.

It was a race he wanted to lose.

Vincent was done running.

I'm coming back for you, Trina.

In no time at all, he was parked outside her apartment

building once more. He practically leaped from the car and sprinted to the entrance.

When he arrived at her door, he hesitated for only a second before knocking urgently, not bothering to check if there was a doorbell somewhere on the wall.

Trina opened the door almost immediately.

Her eyes were red and swollen from crying. Her face, which always had the most contagious of smiles, was drawn. She was still wearing her rain-soaked black dress, a little askew around her body after their kisses.

No matter how she looked, she would always be the most beautiful sight to his eyes.

He couldn't hold back any longer.

The words came out in a torrent of emotion. "I'm sorry for running away, Trina. Maybe I wasn't ready to find out how you really felt. It was something I wasn't prepared for...but it's also something I couldn't run away from. And that's why I'm here."

A sob escaped her throat as she flung herself into his arms, her tears warm as they soaked through his shirt. He held her tightly, feeling the weight of years of unspoken feelings finally pouring out between them.

His voice shook when he spoke, but he didn't care. He was done denying his own feelings, too.

"My heart has always belonged to you," he confessed. "In the racing world, they call me the King of Chains, but you have always been my Queen."

"Vincent," Trina whispered against his chest, "for someone so smart, you're an idiot."

He couldn't help but chuckle at her words, knowing the truth behind them. "I promise I won't run anymore, Trina. I'm here. I'll always be here."

"Good," she murmured, pulling back slightly to look into his eyes. "Don't you dare leave me again. And don't even think about leaving me tonight."

As their lips met in a passionate kiss, he knew he would never leave her side ever again.

Nine
THE TOUCH

After they kissed each other breathless on her threshold, Vincent spoke against her lips.

"No one is leaving tonight, Trina, as long as you tell me this is what you really want."

She nodded.

He smiled as he gently nudged her into the apartment, shutting the door behind them. Once he had closed them off from the rest of the world, he swept her off the floor and laid her down on the couch, covering her body with his.

Oh, god. She could tell what *he* wanted, felt it through those tight black pants that seemed molded to his long legs, as they resumed their heated kissing. Her own body responded as she shifted her hips closer, higher.

She put her hands on his cheeks and stared into his eyes, unable to stop herself from drowning in them. He was fascinating and so deliciously male. Why did she have to look at other men when she had him in front of her the whole time?

"This is what I've always wanted," she whispered. "I'm very

sure."

His lips found hers again. His tongue delved into her mouth as his hands found their way through her clothing. He easily slid the dress off her, followed by her black lace bra and thong.

She had dressed for someone she had never desired, only to be undressed by the one man she had wanted—needed—all this time.

It was worth it, after all, she thought, as she felt him touch that intimate, soaking spot between her legs, felt his mouth close around each of her nipples in turn before making its way down to her heat. She squealed when she felt his tongue on her, her hips bucking wildly. She reached out for him, fumbling with his belt, only to growl and command him to take his clothes off, too.

When he stood bare before her, she marveled at the sheer sight of him. Without clothes, he was more muscle-bound than she'd ever imagined. His tattoos wound around his upper body like chains.

She held out her arms and he went into them. He was very gentle, his voice soft in her ear, promising he would never hurt her. His fingers coaxed her to open, drawing out her pleasure and her need. His lips were on her mouth, on her hair, on her neck, as she ground herself against him, knowing exactly what her body was reaching for.

His timing was exquisite. She felt herself stretch as he entered and sheathed himself inside her. She was the first to move, her hands going up into his hair, her arms locking around his upper back, her teeth grazing his shoulder.

He matched her movements as if they were in a perfectly choreographed dance, his hands on her hips and legs, guiding her body to meet and move against his. He was good, so good.

She felt it then, a warm, snaking sensation beginning to build inside her very core, wrapping itself around her, until she felt it explode between them and send shockwaves of pleasure throughout her body. She heard herself moan his name, followed by incoherent mewls and loud gasps.

"Trina, I love you," he whispered hoarsely, before she felt him tense up and move faster, harder, deeper into her. He made a throaty, guttural sound as his body convulsed on top of hers. She watched pleasure cross his features, savoring how tightly he held on to her, as if for dear life.

She put her arms around him as he slumped on top of her, burying his head between her breasts. She closed her eyes, basking in the bliss that still hummed throughout her body, and the familiar scent and warmth of the man she now had in her arms.

"Vince?" she said into his rumpled hair.

"Yeah?" His eyes were half-closed, his nose nuzzling one breast.

"I'm glad it's you. I've always wanted it to be you."

When she was rewarded by that grin again, and the glitter of what she now recognized as desire in his eyes, she knew they were both in for a long, sleepless night.

In the hours that followed, they explored every corner of her apartment, their bodies coming together in passion and need as they made love over and over again.

From the couch, they rolled down to the living room floor, where he settled her on top of his jacket and put her legs on his shoulders, lifting her hips off the floor as he entered her more deeply than before. She, distantly, heard her loud moans, mixing with his own grunts and groans of pleasure.

With the city lights twinkling through the rain outside the windows, he pressed her against the wall and buried his face between her breasts, their bodies drenched with sweat as they moved and seized pleasure together.

In the kitchen, after they had both eaten more croissants, he devoured her then, using the magic of his tongue, lips and fingers to send her writhing in ecstasy on the tabletop. When he was done, she wrapped her legs around his waist as he took her once more, just as hungrily.

They moved to her bedroom then, where she insisted that she reciprocate what he had done for her in the kitchen. It was then she truly understood how much he really wanted her, and how good he tasted, as he came in her mouth, shouting her name.

In the darkest hours of dawn, their lovemaking became slower, more tender; their earlier desperation and urgency giving way to gentle exploration and intimate confessions.

As the first rays of the sun began to break over the city's skyline, they finally succumbed to exhaustion, collapsing into each other's arms.

As she watched him fall asleep in her embrace, she knew she would never run or hide from him again.

How could she, when her heart had always been his, bound to him with the invisible, unbreakable chains of a love that was there long before she knew it ever existed.

Ten
THE LIGHT

The first thing he realized, when he woke up, was that he wasn't alone in bed.

Vincent found himself looking at long locks of mahogany hair spread out before him. They belonged to the woman sleeping next to him, spooned naked against his body. He still had one arm around her. Her bare buttocks were pressed against his leg.

He slowly reached over to push the hair away from her face. Trina looked beautifully content in sleep. In the morning light, he could see that her pink lips looked slightly swollen.

Morning light.

There was a small digital clock on the nightstand. It read 9:43.

He had overslept by almost five hours, in a bed that wasn't his.

This bed had sheets and pillowcases in white, orange and pink. A peach-colored teddy bear glared at him from its perch next to the digital clock.

So much for his routine.

But this was the kind of Saturday night and Sunday morning he could get used to.

They had made love all over her apartment, and moved to her bedroom afterwards. After savoring all of her, he decided she tasted like mocha, strong and addictive, with an undeniable hint of sweetness.

The last thing he could recall was Trina grinding on top of him, before he turned her over and took her from behind, tantalized by the perfect roundness of her butt the entire time. At some point, they fell asleep, the rain stopped, and the sun rose, in no particular order.

"Good morning." Her voice was sweet, shy, almost girlish. Her eyes were half-open, still a little clouded with sleep.

"Good morning, baby girl," he said, trying out the endearment for the first time in his life. It sounded right. It felt good to say it.

She turned to face him, her arms going around his neck with surprising familiarity. She kissed him square on the lips. "How'd you sleep?"

"Very good. I just woke up, too. I was watching you."

She blushed and buried her face in his neck. "Don't do that."

"Do what?"

"That thing with your eyes."

He had no idea what she was talking about. "Something wrong with my eyes?"

"No. Yes. Whenever you look at me like that, that's it. I'm gone." Understanding slowly dawned on him, as she began nibbling at his neck.

"Trina?" he prompted, tenderly, reaching for her chin.

"Yes?" She settled against the crook of his arm, as comfortably as she would sit in his office.

"What happens to us now?"

She looked at him with surprise in her eyes but said nothing.

He swallowed. He might as well get it over with, before nerves got the better of him.

"Would you like to be my girlfriend? I suppose, sooner rather than later, I would have to propose, too, seeing that we didn't use—"

She giggled, so merrily he forgot any apprehensions he had. She wriggled closer to him. "To all of the above, my answer is yes."

He kissed her soundly. "I love you."

"I love you, too, although I still can't believe I actually fell in love with someone who's secretly an idiot."

He had to laugh. It was refreshing to have his mental faculties taken down a couple of notches, especially when it came to matters of the heart.

She wasn't finished. "My only condition is that you've got to have the energy for this, Mr. Tugade. I don't want to have fun all by myself."

He raised himself up by the elbow and arranged his demeanor into what she called his Presentation Mode.

"Miss David, allow me to show you the real definition of energy. I hope you're ready for a demonstration."

With her laughter washing over him, he plunged into her waiting arms.

BOOK III

Shadow
and
Light

PROLOGUE
THE PRIZED PLAYER

Morning came with a howling wind, the kind that carried dirt and muck that stuck on the skin and never washed out. It seemed to scream in pain.

Arthur gritted his teeth. The storm, gone as quickly as it had come, was over, but everything in the campus was still drenched from the unforgiving intensity of the downpour.

It would be very cold on the field, not to mention muddy. The football pitch looked more like a swamp when he passed by it on his way to the college's main building.

Coach wanted them to start putting in more hours *now*, before first period, for the next intercollegiate football tournament game. Come rain or flood or any other calamity, they would defend their title all the way up to regionals, for the second year in a row.

He descended the steps to the main building's basement. It was a little past six in the morning. The prized player's first class started at eight and now he was most probably in his lair, practicing those deft knee tricks that brought tears to the eyes of the rival coaches.

As team captain, it was Arthur's job to secure the gear and

inform the prized player about that morning's practice not getting cancelled in spite of the field's condition.

Not that he'd care either way, he thought bitterly

The prized player was a tireless machine, not a person. He'd show up, do the drills and rounds, and commit the plays to memory. Arthur often wondered what possessed him to turn down the position of captain, after bringing the team to two regional championships since he was a freshman.

Even as a senior, Arthur was only the distant second choice to lead the team this year. His numbers in goals and successful plays were pathetic compared to the prized player's, as was everyone else's. The man pretty much did not miss goals.

He typed in the door code and stepped inside the basement, which housed a collection of old school furniture and relatively new sports equipment. He knocked on the door of a smaller room inside, once a storage closet for cleaning equipment and a break room for campus cleaning staff, before the lay-offs.

This was now the prized player's residence on campus, because he didn't want to share his space with three other kids in the dormitory next door.

No answer. Arthur turned the knob, finding it unlocked, and pushed warily.

There was nothing in the prized player's room except a sparse wooden cot, an equally drab three-legged table, and a portable clothes rack.

The team helped him load back the equipment only last night, he thought. *Knowing him, he wouldn't move out of this place. It's his lion's den, after all.*

Arthur knew that the prized player had some other stuff around, like dartboards, target posters, and sketches of exotic birds. They were all gone. Nothing was draped on the makeshift clothesline strung across the tiny room.

He stood there and assessed this new information for half a minute.

Arthur took a deep breath and closed the door. He retraced his steps in the basement, retrieving two footballs from the storage racks before he left.

He had better tell Coach that Aragon was gone.

ACT 1
Falling

ONE

THE DARK

*I*t was dark.

In his world, somehow, it always seemed dark.

He gingerly lowered his body onto a lopsided stone bench overlooking the quad. His muscles ached and his sides burned from the run.

The campus was still cloaked in the night. He had been running for more than an hour, but the sky still resembled a blue-black canopy strewn with thick masses of clouds. Not a ray of sunlight breached his limited view of the horizon; it was still too early for that. The air was thick and heavy, and sullied by city dust.

Rain was coming.

He felt a detached, perverse satisfaction.

"Aragon?"

A female voice had said his family name. People knew him by that name.

Aragon.

A name full of history. His place of birth was far enough away, but he could still recollect the smells of gunpowder, the crisp click of a gun's hammer, the echo of death cries. They all came with his heritage.

His well-trained eyes made out her silhouette. The lighting in the campus was limited and the few functional lampposts badly needed their bulbs replaced.

"Jeri." Her name fell from his lips. After all this time, he was still surprised at the way he would say it. Softer, slower than his usual speech, and always with awe.

She was dressed in a white top and a denim skirt. The balmy breeze played with the strands of her long, wavy hair. She carried a black backpack, the size of which dwarfed her frame.

He wasn't surprised to feel his chest tighten, his heartbeat accelerate. "What are you doing here? How did you get in the campus?"

He watched her place the bag on the concrete pavement and take a seat beside him.

"I had to see you," she replied simply.

"How did you get in?" he pressed.

He lived on campus, in the main building's basement. He had first lodged in a boarding house, then moved to the dormitory after he'd secured a permanent spot in the college's varsity football team. He was not comfortable with the noise and activity in shared living spaces.

Coach had allowed him to hole up in the old janitors' break room, right next to the storage where the sports teams kept all their equipment. The old man could not refuse the simple request of the college's star athlete and pulled every string he could with Administration to make this strange request happen.

"Being in the Student Council has its benefits." There was a smile in her voice. "I couldn't sleep. I figured you would be here."

"I couldn't sleep, either."

Jeri slid onto the bench next to him. He opened his arms and she snuggled into them. She pressed her face to his chest, not minding his sweat-soaked shirt.

"I really missed you." Her voice was a melodious whisper in the stillness. "It's been so busy with your game and the debates…"

"I missed you, too. A lot."

The confession was a rare display of boldness in terms of expressing how he felt. This was a first for him, and he did it only for her.

"I wanted to call you earlier, but I knew you'd be sleeping," he went on as he touched her hair, wrapping the smooth strands around his rough palm. The contrast was undeniably appealing. "As always, the best option is to run. Wait it out until the sun finally decides to come up."

She giggled. "You're crazy, Aragon."

He had to smile at her declaration, knowing that the only witnesses were the darkness and her. "Maybe I am, because you're here with me and you're so fucking beautiful."

Her giggles dissolved into a breathless sigh as he leaned in for a kiss. Their lips met tentatively at first, before melding together with a passion that no amount of repetition or familiarity could dull.

As their kiss deepened, he found his hands on her body, his fingers hungrily reaching for the softness and curves under her blouse.

She was in a similar state, her hands pulling at his hair as she pressed her body closer and tighter against his, practically melting into his heated skin.

"Crazy," she repeated, this time in a low growl.

"Come with me," he murmured against her lips. He stood up and took her bag, then held out a hand to her.

Wordlessly and without hesitation, she took it, her eyes wide and luminous in the semi-darkness.

He led her to his living quarters, their own little private sanctuary for more than a year now. When they were together, everything else held little consequence.

In those moments, she was the only one who mattered.

As soon as the locked door shut out the rest of the world, his lips found hers again, gently, but quickly growing more demanding and urgent.

He lost himself in the taste and feel of her, always reminding him of the tart sweetness of apples. It was something he could never get enough of.

For someone who had been taught his entire life not to get too attached to anyone or anything, he knew he had already lost this battle to her, long before he'd ever known what it was he felt for her.

The memory of the first time he saw her was striking in its simplicity and unforgettable in its intensity.

That day remained etched in his memory, the mark it made deeper than any of the arcane teachings that had been repeatedly drilled into him over the years.

From that day on, he knew, somehow, that he'd always belonged to the woman in his arms.

TWO

The Orientation Week of freshman year at the university dawned cloudy and rainy, perhaps an omen of things to come.

He was a stranger to most of the people around him, more so than usual, even in the boarding house where he stayed. He was surrounded by students from other provinces, but he still stood out like a sore thumb, with his accent and his reputation.

He'd been uprooted from the south, on a full football scholarship. The name Aragon had already made its way all over the country, a football player who had never experienced defeat on the field during his elementary and high school years. The universities had fought over him. He'd chosen this particular one because it was the farthest away.

He left his accommodation very early that day and spent the morning practicing on the field, alone, in the middle of the rain. He had a few hours before the start of orientation; he might as well do something useful. Any kind of training was beneficial.

The rain stopped and the sun broke through the clouds just in time for the freshman events to start. At the college auditorium, he joined the queue of new students quietly, hoping he wouldn't get noticed or singled out.

In sharp contrast to his desire to blend in, Jeri was one of the few brave souls who volunteered to be the freshman batch representative.

He watched her ascend the stage with grace and determination, her gaze sweeping over the crowd before settling on the microphone. Her smile was radiant and genuine. She had thick, dark brown hair that tumbled over her shoulders in waves, framing her round face like a halo.

"Hello, everyone," she began, her voice clear and melodic. "My name is Jerann Castelo, but you can call me Jeri. I'm here today because I believe in a better future for all of us, a future where every student has the opportunity to shine and achieve great things, no matter where each of us came from."

No matter where each of us came from.

He was struck and captivated by her words and the passion behind them.

The rest of her speech rang clearly, sincerely. "What is more important is where we are headed and what we can accomplish along the way. We can do this together if we help and support one another, starting today: right here, right now."

She possessed a magnetism that drew him in, the way her intelligent brown eyes seemed to pierce through his very core, seeing him for what he truly was. She had the gaze of a predator, but it was also warm and welcoming. It was a dangerous, intoxicating combination, one she was probably not even aware of.

It was no wonder she won with a decisive margin; she was a force of nature, a beacon of light.

He thought of her like the sun, a radiant star that burned brightly. It was a stark contrast to the shadows in which he had been trained to dwell, a nameless weapon cloaked in secrecy and anonymity.

Her presence wrapped around him like an embrace. It was

a strange, but not unwelcome, sensation, one he got just by looking at a girl who stood and spoke on the podium.

He'd been taught to suppress emotions, to sever all ties to the world around him in order to survive.

Looking at Jeri Castelo challenged all of that.

He mustered the courage to speak with her, to his credit—or perhaps to his doom.

The auditorium was abuzz with excitement as the newly-elected freshman representative descended the stage after the announcements of the college dean.

"Congratulations, Jeri," he said, sidling up to her amid the throngs of students offering their well-wishes. His heart hammered in his chest, unaccustomed to such vulnerability with another person, but her smile eased the tension effortlessly.

"Thank you," she replied. "I appreciate it, uh..?"

"N—" He almost said his name in response, but before he could, a group of adoring girls and boys descended upon her, their voices clamoring for attention.

They'd apparently known her from her high school debate days, and their admiration was palpable in the air that crackled with energy and enthusiasm.

"Hey, Jeri! Remember us?" one of them called out. "We were in the Science High School across the road from you. We had an event on international trade policies."

And just like that, she was swept away by the tide of her admirers, leaving him standing alone in the crowded auditorium.

After that, he always watched her from afar, his gaze following her as she moved through the campus like a whirlwind. She gave him the regulation blue booklets for their quizzes twice during freshman year, whenever he forgot to buy them—the first time for a History exam, the second for an essay assignment in PE he had to write down fifteen minutes before the class started. He was particularly desperate on both occasions, and she graciously came to his rescue.

Her sunny presence was a constant in his life, shining on him brightly even as he retreated further into the shadows the more people paid attention to him and asked questions about his life before university.

He only ever stepped out of the shadows when it was time to play.

On the football field, he could be exactly as he was, without inhibitions or hesitation. While the ball was in play, he could assert his control, bend his body to his will, outsmart and outrun his opponents.

It was the only time he could let go.

He wished he could let go, too, when it came to what he felt for the girl whose presence he craved almost obsessively.

Sometimes, in the early evenings, he would see her seated alone under the fire tree in the campus quad, the bright blossoms a vibrant contrast to her pensive expression. There was a heaviness in her posture, a burden that seemed to weigh her down as she stared off into the distance, lost in thought.

It was in those moments, when the world around them turned momentarily insignificant, that he saw himself reflected in her eyes.

He wanted to reach out, to bridge the gap between them, but fear held him back—fear of rejection, of inadequacy, of the consequences that came with letting someone in, after so many years of being taught to do the exact opposite.

He did try, one time, at the start of their sophomore year, when she was running for a spot at the University Student Council.

It was dusk, but he knew she was not even halfway done with the day.

She was seated on a stone bench overlooking the quad, as usual, surrounded by a hefty stack of books and the large backpack she carried all over campus. It was a wonder how her petite frame managed to stay upright and even walk around.

It was now or never. He had to take the shot.

Before he could overthink the entire matter of approaching her, he found himself standing next to the bench.

"Hi, Jeri."

He was painfully aware that he cast a shadow over her. Swallowing hard, he stepped out of the way of what little light there was left before the sun completely set.

"Oh, hi." She looked up with a tentative, hesitant smile.

An involuntary shiver ran down his spine as their eyes met. An irrational thought struck him.

Does she know?

He didn't even know what to say. When he thought about it, the only thing he had in common with her was that they were both sophomores—and they had one class together that semester, Philosophy.

He said the only thing that came to mind as he took in the sheer amount of belongings around her. "May I sit with you?"

She made space for him by putting her books in her lap. "Sure. Can I help with you something? Is this about Math 100?"

He took a seat, careful to keep a respectful distance. "Math 100?"

She nodded. "I've been asked a lot lately about tutoring people in Calculus."

"No, not about Math 100, although I would appreciate the help if you've got the time."

Her smile was kind, but he couldn't help but notice the dark circles under her eyes, the drawn expression on her face despite the genuine light in her gaze.

"I'll have a look at my schedule at the Learning Center, but I'd be happy to slot you in if there are still free spots left."

"Thanks."

Silence fell over them, awkward and heavy.

He didn't know where he got the guts to speak first.

"I just wanted to ask if you're okay. I was passing by and, well, I noticed you've been looking a little…overwhelmed lately."

She studied him intently before saying anything in response. "Am I that transparent?" He wasn't sure if she laughed or sighed. "I guess I didn't realize anyone was paying attention."

"It's hard not to notice when someone's constantly on the move, always pushing themselves to do more."

She looked away, tightening her arms around her books.

He drew back, afraid he had offended her.

"Yeah, well, I've got a lot riding on this year," she finally said, looking back at him with a stiff grin. "I can't afford to slow down."

He doubted the sincerity of her words, but he knew he was in no position to question someone like Jeri Castelo. He chose not to say anything, shifting slightly in his seat to make a quick getaway before he inflicted any further damage. As he did, his shoulder brushed against hers. Her skin felt warm even through the worn material of his shirt

"I don't look okay, do I, Aragon?"

Her candid, murmured declaration was a surprise. He chose his next words carefully. "You don't have to carry the weight of the world on your shoulders, you know. There will always be someone who's willing to help. You've always helped everyone. It's your turn now."

She looked at him for a long stretch of time before speaking. "You make it sound so easy and straightforward. I guess that's what makes you such a great team player."

He was inexplicably flattered to know that she'd watched him play.

"Thanks."

"You're welcome. I guess I just need to find my balance, with everything that's been going on. It's too late to turn back once I'm committed to something."

"I know what you mean."

She glanced at her watch and sighed. "It's time for me to go. I've got Economics at six."

She made a move to stand up. Before he realized what he was doing, his hand was on her arm.

"Can I help you with those?" He gestured to the hulking backpack and pile of books between them.

Wide-eyed, she nodded. "Sure."

He needed no further prompting or instruction. He slung the bag over his shoulder and relieved her of the books.

"Are you sure it's fine with you? You're not off to practice or anywhere else, are you? I don't want to trouble you, honestly."

He shook his head and, for the first time in what seemed like the longest time, attempted a smile.

"It's okay. Happy to help."

He followed her across the quad and to the classroom.

"Thanks, Aragon," she said as soon as they reached the entrance.

"Anytime." It wasn't lost on him how the other students in the classroom stared.

"I owe you one. I'll let you know if I've still got that free Calculus slot, okay?"

She gave his forearm a squeeze before she turned and made her way into the room. Her touch felt like a white-hot brand on his skin.

"Sure," he replied to her retreating back. "See you around, Jeri."

The erratic pounding of his heart was strange to his ears. Even his breathing pattern had changed, just by being in close proximity to her.

If only you could show me what you really are, he said to her, silently, watching as she joined the others and once more changed into the vivacious girl everyone in the college was familiar with.

If only you could see me for what I really am, too.

If only we could let each other in.

THREE

THE DISTANCE

His resolve held for a week, at best. After that, he knew he couldn't stay away from her.

Exactly seven days after they spoke on the quad, he found himself waiting outside Jeri's Economics classroom, carefully concealed beneath the shadows of a tree.

As soon as the final bell of the evening rang, she emerged from the classroom, as vibrant as ever, with an entourage of classmates from her political party. They were all laden down with campaign posters, her photograph beaming from all of them.

He wanted to approach her, to talk to her some more, but her companions commanded her full attention. He hesitated, uncomfortable with the idea of others observing their interaction. This was unknown territory to him; the presence of other people made him uneasy. He'd just as soon lose his nerve.

Instead, he opted to wait for her to finish, planning to offer to walk her home. Over the past year, he'd sometimes caught glimpses of her walking on the streets surrounding the university. She probably lived nearby.

He watched her and her team as they dispersed to cover

different areas of the college. He chose to remain hidden, waiting for the perfect moment to step out of the shadows.

It was late in the evening when Jeri finally left the campus, laden down with her bag and books. With her head high and shoulders back as if she owned the world, her determined stride carried her towards the residential area. He tried to close the gap between them, hoping that she would see him and maybe even smile in recognition. Something held him back, an invisible barrier he couldn't bring himself to breach.

He knew what it was, at the back of his mind, although his pride would never allow him to speak of it.

Fear.

It was the same feeling he had a week ago, moments before he'd approached her on the quad.

Instead, he followed her from a safe distance, his eyes never leaving her as she approached the less crowded parts of the neighborhood. His thoughts raced, wondering how she would react if she knew he was trailing her like some sort of stalker. He'd been trained to recon and observe unnoticed, and now he used those skills only to see her safely home.

That was it, wasn't it?

To make sure she was safe.

As Jeri walked deeper into the dimly lit streets, his senses heightened. The sound of laughter reached his ears, quickly morphing into something far more sinister. The air grew thick with tension, and his pulse quickened in response.

"Hey there, cutie pie," a gruff voice called out, the words dripping with menace. Four men emerged from the shadows of an alley, surrounding her. "We just want your laptop and your phone, and you can be on your way."

She clutched her belongings to her chest. "Please," she begged, her voice breaking. "I need these for school. I'll give you my money, but please, let me keep my things."

The thugs laughed cruelly at her plight. "You're running for the Student Council, aren't you? You're very famous, even in these parts. You should be able to afford new ones."

His heart twisted; his breath hitched. It wasn't in preparation for the kill. It was something more raw and far less calculating.

It was an overwhelming sense of anger, heavily laced with concern. It drove him to admit that he could no longer remain a passive observer.

He couldn't stay in the shadows now.

She needed him.

It took him a single step to come out into the light, radiating from a nearby streetlamp. "Leave her alone."

The men turned their attention to him, their eyes sizing him up. Beneath their predatory sneers, he could sense their hesitation, an uncertainty in confronting a stranger who dared to stand up to them.

And he wasn't just any stranger.

"Who the fuck do you think you are, college boy?" one of the thugs growled.

"Someone who won't let you hurt her." His tone didn't waver as he felt Jeri's gaze upon him. He counted two knives, one retractable steel baton. The biggest of the men, in all likelihood their leader, didn't display any weapons. The leader probably carried a piece, too, but it didn't matter. They were nothing to him.

"Fine," snarled the biggest man, stepping closer to him with a menacing grin. "We'll just take care of you first."

As the leader lunged towards him, he reacted with barely a thought. His fighting style, as old as time, was subtle, fluid, like water flowing around an obstacle. There was no brute force in his movements, no unnecessary exertion of strength. It was as if he were simply stepping out of their way, guiding their own momentum against them.

"Fuck you!" the leader howled as he crumpled to the ground, clutching at an incapacitated arm. The others stared, momentarily stunned by the ease with which their companion had been defeated.

He didn't give any of them time to recover, or even express their regret at mugging Jeri or challenging him. It took him twelve moves to take the remaining three of them down. It would have taken nine had he wanted to go for the kill.

But she was there, watching him.

In mere moments, all four thugs lay sprawled on the pavement, with fractured bones and egos. They scrambled to their feet, their faces twisted with fear and pain, before fleeing into the shadows.

He stood silently, breathing his way back into a calmer state, before he spoke to her.

"Are you okay, Jeri?"

She nodded wordlessly, still clutching her books tightly to her body. Her eyes were wide, filled with residual fear mixed with gratitude and relief.

"Here. Let me take your things."

She offered no resistance when he moved to relieve her of her backpack and gently pulled the books out of her death grip.

"How...how did you get here?" Her voice was trembling, a far cry from her usual confident manner of speech. "It's so late."

"Football practice ran late. I was just on my way to grab some food when I saw you."

He was relieved when she didn't pry further.

"Thank you," she said quietly, barely above a whisper. "I...I don't know what could have happened if you weren't around. I could have l-lost everything. And I've worked so hard, too..."

Her voice trailed off, as if she'd seemingly stopped herself from saying too much.

"You're welcome." He thought it was the safest, most neutral response. "Do you live nearby? I've seen you walking this way a few times before."

"My grandparents live a couple of blocks away. Most of the time I walk to school." Her voice shook slightly. In the lamplight, he could see the hint of unshed tears in her eyes.

He could easily deal with four armed men, with his bare hands, but not with something like this. He didn't have the training to deal with an oncoming assault of emotions and tears.

He swallowed hard. "Can you walk? I'll take you home. Would that be okay?"

She nodded and, to his surprise, inched closer to him. He could feel her body heat, could see her flushed cheeks.

"Would you like to take my arm?" he offered, not sure why he did. It felt right to say it.

She accepted without hesitation. He didn't mind the weight of her things at all; he was very conscious of how close she was as they slowly made their way through the darkened streets, her hand resting lightly on his forearm. She smelled of something fruity and warm.

"This has never happened to me before," she said softly. "I know this neighborhood and most of the people around. I've lived here since I was seven."

"I'm very sorry this happened to you, Jeri."

"It's fine. It's a good thing you're here."

She stopped walking and let go of his arm when they reached a modest two-story house with yellow wood panels and a red galvanized-iron roof, nestled in a lane of similar-looking houses. "Well, this is me."

He took his phone out of his pocket and gave it to her. "Here. Please put your number in."

She took the phone wordlessly and typed in the digits as requested. As she did, she looked up midway through the task, twice, eyeing him curiously. As their eyes met, something stirred within him—an unfamiliar, yet somehow welcome, emotion.

She handed the phone back and he called her, waiting for her phone to ring. It played a beautifully melodious ballad, crooned by a woman with a haunting voice.

"That's a nice song."

"It's called *'Building a Mystery,'* by Sarah McLachlan," she said, as she took her phone out of her pocket to cut the call. "It's been around for a while, but I really like it."

He glanced at the dimly-lit house before him and back at her. "Promise me you'll call if you ever need anything. I'll be there."

"Really, I don't want to bother you. You've done more than enough and I—"

"Please, Jeri. Promise me." The imploring tone he heard in his voice was surprising even to his own ears.

"Okay. I promise."

A sense of relief coursed through him. He hoped she hadn't said it just to get rid of him.

"I guess I should be on my way."

Before he could react, she put her hand on his shoulder and tiptoed to kiss the lower part of his left cheek, her lips only able to reach as high as his jawline.

He felt like he'd caught fire, the contact leaving a searing heat as if she'd pressed a blowtorch right on the spot where her mouth was mere seconds ago.

"I guess." She took a step back and held out her hands. "Be careful, okay?"

He stared at her uncertainly for several long seconds.

Fuck.

Was he supposed to hug her now, or maybe kiss her back? Not that he didn't want to. He'd wanted to since he first saw her but…

"My things, please?"

Heat rushed up his neck and suffused his face, making him grateful for the cover of night. Heart pounding, he carefully handed over her backpack and books, hoping she wouldn't see that his hands were actually trembling.

"There you go. Good night, Jeri."

"Good night."

With a nod, he turned away from her and began to retrace his steps to the campus. In truth, he still hadn't eaten anything since lunch, but now—

"Nick?"

Her voice carried quietly down the empty street.

Nick.

His first name was Nicholas, but none of his peers ever called him by it. Only the teachers who called the roll ever did.

He was Aragon to people in the university and this city.

She didn't even use his complete given name. Just Nick, as if she'd known him all her life.

He looked over his shoulder to see her still standing in front of the house, looking at him dead on.

"What is it?"

"Thank you. I'll never forget this."

He turned to face her, pushing his hands into his pockets to prevent them from doing something stupid—like close the distance between them again and take her in his arms.

He hesitated before launching into the question he'd really wanted to ask. "Can you do me a favor then?"

"Anything."

"Can we keep this between us? I don't want people to make a fuss."

"I understand. You can trust me."

He nodded. "Thanks, Jeri. I'll see you tomorrow."

"See you tomorrow, Nick."

His walk back to the campus was a blur, the idea of dinner losing its appeal the more he thought of what had just happened.

The fight, if one could even call it that.

The first time he'd shown an outsider even just a tiny glimpse of the true extent of his abilities.

The kiss.

The first time a girl had put her lips anywhere near him.

The promise.

The first time he had willingly offered his protection to someone without a price.

The name.

Nick. Spoken as if it were the most normal thing in the world for her to do.

He didn't realize he was already within the university's walls. He pulled out his phone, holding on to it tightly, as if it was tethered to the girl who was now hopefully safe and secure blocks away.

He took a deep breath and dialed her number. As he listened to the ringing sound, he felt tight knots form in his stomach, only to loosen when he finally heard her pick up at the other end.

"Hello, Nick?" she answered hesitantly.

"Hey, I'm sorry to bother you. I just wanted to check on you."

"Thank you," she breathed. "I'm…I'm fine. Just a little shaken, that's all. But I should be okay. I'm just getting ready for bed. What about you? Did you get any dinner?"

"Ah, it's fine," he replied, glancing at the deserted quad around him. "I'll be off to the gym soon."

"Really?" she sounded incredulous. "Do you ever sleep at all?"

He didn't answer, evading the question with a subtle deflection. "I'm just glad you're okay, Jeri."

"Well, I owe you one. I'll bring something nice for you to eat tomorrow to make it up to you. I'm so sorry you missed dinner."

"Please, don't worry about it," he insisted, uncomfortable at the thought of someone going out of their way for him.

They spoke briefly about her campaign, and he couldn't help but admit that he would vote only for her, despite there being two available spots on the University Student Council.

"Your support means a lot." Her voice was now lighter, less tense. The more relaxed she sounded, the better he felt, too. "But I have to say, it's because of you that our university is back on the sporting map. It's like you've proven to the entire region that we're not just a bunch of nerds with our noses buried in books."

As their conversation continued, she asked about his well-being, if he needed anything or if there was any way she could help him, so far from home. The genuine concern in her voice moved him, and he understood why she was so beloved by everyone at school.

As they spoke, he walked to the bench on the quad where Jeri usually sat and assumed her place under the shelter of the tree. When they finally exchanged goodbyes and he waited for her to cut the call first, he realized it was barely an hour before midnight.

He stared down at his phone as if it could provide answers to the swirling questions in his mind.

What did he really feel for her?

Did she have any idea about it? What would she think of him if she knew?

What was he going to do about any of it, as someone living on borrowed time?

The stillness of the night wrapped around him heavily. Most students would have been fast asleep by now, but sleep rarely came easy to him.

As he entered the dimly lit gym adjacent to the auditorium, he took a deep breath, inhaling the familiar scent of sweat and rusted steel that permeated the air. This was his sanctuary, a place where he could lose himself in his training and forget, if only for a little while, the real weight of his dual existence.

With each precise strike against the punching bag, each rep of the heavy barbells only he could lift, he tried to push all thought out of his mind, focusing only on the screaming of his muscles.

But thoughts of her persisted, even as he tried to punch and kick harder than usual, lift heavier than he normally would.

He paused in his training, pressing his face to the cold and grimy wall, trying to ignore the hunger that raged in his stomach.

"Damn it," he muttered under his breath, slamming his fist against the wall in frustration. The pain that lanced through his hand was a welcome distraction.

He needed not to think about time, about how he couldn't take it back no matter how strong he became, how hard he trained, or how much determination he possessed.

Time was his greatest enemy. He had already used up more than a year of it; he had less than three left.

Three years was nothing. It would all flash by in a heartbeat, and he would be dead again.

He was fighting a losing battle.

But he wasn't going down easily.

FOUR

THE DIVIDE

He found out they were both creatures of habit.

That small snippet of realization took down one more piece of the wall around him, as he unknowingly began to let her in.

The day after he'd walked her home for the first time, Jeri brought him a meticulously packed bundle of food: steamed rice, small cuts of grilled meat, and a piece of fruit. She turned up at the corner of the field right after the team's morning practice session. She repeated this the following day, this time with a small container of stir-fried noodles and vegetables clutched in her hands.

She became his tutor in Calculus, too, in twice-weekly sessions they spent in a corner desk just outside the library. Away from the confines of the Learning Center and the strict silence of the stacks, the spot always seemed reserved for her. Once he'd asked her if she'd signed him up officially as a tutee; she'd just shrugged and smiled.

He became, unofficially, her shadow. He walked her home almost every day, especially on those times when she stayed on campus until late in the evening. Even on days when football practice was supposed to drain him of energy, he found himself accompanying her on the darkened streets, seeing her safely to the yellow house with the red roof, which always seemed devoid of life.

As the days flew by, they became part of each other's daily routines.

Shortly before the University Student Council elections, he picked her up from her Economics class. They were once again subjected to curious stares, this time a little more openly. He wondered how she could live with such scrutiny every day.

"Hi." Jeri appeared at the doorway of the classroom, greeting him with a small smile.

"Ready for some Calculus?" He extended a hand, knowing she understood what he meant.

She turned over her backpack without question. "Always. Let's get you ready for a great score during the mid-terms. That way you won't have to stress so much on the finals."

They walked across the quad to their usual spot outside the library. As the night deepened, they delved into derivatives and integrals, her patience with him as saintly as her presence was soothing.

They were packing up their things when she hesitated before leaving the library building.

"I've been meaning to tell you," she said hesitantly, stopping on top of the steps that led to the quad outside. "I didn't want to talk about it before, but I thought you should know."

"What is it?"

Were people talking about him, to her? What did they know?

She averted her eyes from his before speaking, clutching her books to her chest and belly. This was her self-preservation reflex, using her books to protect her vital organs.

It was strangely endearing.

"Ever since we started spending time together, my campaign has picked up. People are taking notice, especially the sororities.

I've gotten two invitations to pledge in the past week. They thought, well, that I'm your girlfriend." She swallowed hard and looked him in the eye. "I'm so sorry."

"Why?" He held on to her gaze as he relieved her of the books. She need not worry about anything hurting her, as long as he was around.

"Why what?"

"Why are you sorry, Jeri?"

She bit her lip and shook her head. "I don't know. For people misinterpreting our friendship, I guess. I just don't want you to think I'm using you or anything."

"Using me?"

"You're practically a celebrity in this school, Nick. Anyone close to you would have a higher clout than they'd ever have on their own. That includes me."

Had he been someone else, he would have laughed at the ridiculousness of the idea. But he could sense her anxiety, her fear of being misunderstood.

He didn't know the first thing about politics, but fear was something he understood intimately.

"How can you use me, when I'm doing all of this by choice?"

"Are you really?"

He nodded.

He wasn't even finished with his response before he found himself, laden down with her backpack and her books, in her arms.

She was hugging him. It was awkward and lopsided, but he didn't care.

"I don't care what people think," he said, uncertain on how to respond using his actions. He couldn't even move that much.

She gave him a squeeze before letting go. "Thanks. You're a really great guy, you know."

He felt a mixture of relief and loss once she broke contact.

"Alright. Okay, let's get going."

The walk to her house was quiet and leisurely, with a few snippets of conversation in between; they talked about the start of the intercollegiate sports season, about the upcoming elections.

Life, for a while, was simple.

When they reached her house, Jeri hesitated at the gate as he handed over her things. She went on tiptoe as before. This time, he bent down so she could reach his cheek properly.

"That's better," she murmured against his skin before kissing him. "Thanks, Nick."

As soon as the books were in her grip, it was his turn to put his arms around her.

For the first time in his life, he hugged a girl.

He could feel the slight tremble in her body. She was wonderfully soft and warm to the touch.

"Good night, Jeri."

With her hands occupied, she leaned into him, her face nestling against the crook of his neck. "Good night. See you tomorrow."

As he walked away, the distance between them growing wider with each step, he felt the familiar buzz of his phone in his pocket.

Barely a moment had passed since their goodbye, and already she had sent him a message.

He was about to text her back when the world around him shifted, a sudden chill creeping up his spine.

He was no longer alone.

Eight shadows materialized around him, some of their faces

familiar. Half of them were part of the same group of men who had mugged Jeri weeks back.

This time, however, three of them brandished guns. The metal shone dully under the dim glow of the streetlights.

"Go back to whichever hell you came from, hero."

He recognized the leader, feeling a sudden pang of sympathy for him. If the would-be gangster thought he could save face, he was in for another disappointment.

An icy calm settled over him as he assessed the situation, his mind racing with possible strategies and outcomes like a high-speed game of chess.

He stared at the barrel of the gun closest to him. His voice was steady when he spoke. "Over my dead body."

The men laughed, their jeers echoing through the empty streets.

"If you think the tricks you used to impress your little girlfriend would work on us, you're fucking wrong, kid."

"Those tricks worked very well the first time. I can still remember how quickly you hit the ground."

"You're such a smartass, aren't you, college boy?"

"Just telling the truth." His jaw clenched as he inhaled deeply, drawing on his years of training to center himself before a fight.

He knew he shouldn't be doing this. He'd traveled so far to get away from it all, and yet here he was, letting himself get dragged right back into a world of violence. It was a vicious circle, one he couldn't seem to escape.

The fight broke out with a sudden ferocity, but he saw everything unfold in painfully slow motion. His fists connected with jaws and torsos, bones shattering under the force of his blows. He wove through the group of men, ducking beneath wild punches and countering with devastating precision. It was almost as if he had never left, the muscle memory of countless sparring sessions and battles awakening within him.

The fight raged on outside, but inside him settled a numbing realization. As he sidestepped and countered attacks around him, he accepted the inescapable truth: a normal life was never truly meant for him.

He was, after all, Cain.

Twin to death, forged in blood.

As he battled the men, dodged their knives and bullets with an almost insulting ease, he understood that as long as he lingered in the shadows, violence would continue to claw at him, always demanding to be acknowledged.

And so he lunged forward, disarming two of the men of their guns in one fluid, practiced motion. The cold weight of the weapons settled into his palms, feeling both alien and familiar all at once. They were imitation guns; cheap, soldered versions of the perfectly balanced Glocks he usually favored.

Fake gun or not, it would be so easy to pull the trigger, as natural to him as breathing. For a brief moment, he considered it.

Instead of aiming for the sweet spot between their eyes, as he had been trained to do, he shifted his aim, targeting the knees of the men before him. The gunshots rang out like muffled thunder, encrusted in rusty shells.

"Stay away from me and the girl." He stared down the last man standing, who still clutched his imitation gun with trembling hands.

"Or what?" the man challenged, a desperate defiance in his eyes.

Without hesitation, he fired again, the bullet tearing through the gunman's fingers, wrenching the weapon from his grip. Blood splattered on the grimy, trash-littered pavement as he turned away, as quickly as he had finished the fight.

He knew he had to move fast. Someone would have heard the shots, no matter how late in the night it was. Someone would investigate. It was only a matter of time.

With a heavy sigh, he bent down and collected the weapons

of the fallen men, their moans and curses a grim soundtrack to his calculated actions. He found one of them wearing a fairly large jacket; he kicked the man over and ripped the jacket off him, using the fabric as a makeshift bundle for the guns and blades he'd gathered.

Moving with laser focus, he found an empty alley a few blocks away, just around the corner from the university. He entered the darkened area cautiously, ensuring he was alone before getting to work.

He didn't need light to guide his hands as he disassembled the fake guns and broke the blades off the knives' hilts. Using his powerful left leg, he kicked open a nearby manhole, the metallic clang setting his teeth on edge.

One by one, he dropped the pieces of his handiwork into the drainage, watching as they disappeared into the murky sewage below. The darkness swallowed the remnants of his violent encounter.

He was the only one who remained, aside from the eight men and their broken bodies. If they wanted a third round, he would gladly give it to them. This time, none of them would be walking away.

As he made his way back towards the university, the distant sound of police sirens pierced the night air.

His reaction to the sound was a first: his heart pounded in his chest, mingling with a rush of adrenaline and fear through his veins. In the past, he wouldn't have cared about the consequences—escaping and disappearing into the shadows would have been second nature to him.

But, now, things had changed.

Jeri.

With her long brown hair and equally dark eyes, with her smile and sweet little kisses. She'd hugged him earlier, hadn't she?

She'd brought him food every day, too, yet another burden

for her to carry.

A random thought crossed his mind as he made his way through the darkened quad, his gaze brushing past the bench where she usually sat in the late afternoons.

More than half the books she always carried were not for her. They were for the people she tutored, including him.

The thought of being apart from her caused him physical pain, a gnawing sensation that ate its way from inside his chest.

He couldn't leave now.

He couldn't ever leave her.

Upon reaching his room, he sank onto the bed, his heart still racing. No amount of breathing techniques seemed to work in calming it down.

He knew there was only one way to deal with it.

He picked up his phone with trembling hands, skinned and bloodied from the fight, and dialed her number.

She picked up after four rings, her voice groggy when she answered. "Hello, Nick?"

"Hi, Jeri," he said softly. "I'm back on campus."

Something about his response must have sounded off to her. Her next words were more alert. "Are you okay? Have you eaten anything?"

The answer to both was a resounding no, but he didn't have to tell her. He hesitated for a moment, then forced a smile into his voice. "Yeah, I'm fine. I just wanted to say good night."

"Are you sure you're okay? Why don't you have some of those sandwiches I brought earlier? You haven't eaten them all yet, have you?"

The white plastic container with the green cover was on the tiny table next to him, already empty. Ever since she'd started bringing him food, he would wash those pieces of Tupperware religiously and returned them to her, squeaky clean and spotless, the following day.

"I have a few pieces left, thanks." He hoped the lightness he affected in his tone was enough not to make her any more concerned. "You're a lifesaver."

"I'll get some more food to you in the morning, okay? I'm so sorry our session ran late. Next time you don't have to worry about walking me home. Everyone at school will kill me if anything happens to you. Your coach will probably string me up on the flagpole."

"Nothing like that's going to happen," he assured her, cringing as the sterile fluorescent lights illuminated the torn, uneven skin on his knuckles. He'd have to make up some excuse about the punching bag ripping, then he'd have to rip the real thing convincingly. "I'm perfectly fine. I just wanted to say good night."

"Um…Nick?"

"Yeah?"

"Promise me you'll let me take care of you. You're so far from home and you're always doing something the rest of us can only dream about."

He didn't answer. He stared at the phone, as if she was speaking in a foreign language he didn't understand.

"Hello?"

"I'm here."

I'll always be here.

He desperately wanted to tell her how he really felt.

He was scared and lonely, hungry for her touch just as much as his body craved sustenance. He was hurting inside and out, his limbs reeling from the exertions of his grueling training routine on and off the field, from the fight he could have easily ended with well-placed gunshots.

Most of all, he really wanted to be with her.

If only for a short while.

"You promise, right?"

"Right."

She paused. He thought perhaps she wasn't satisfied with his answer. She was, after all, a very intelligent person. It would only be a matter of time before she saw right through his lies.

He was relieved when she finally said something. "You sure you're okay?"

"Yeah. I'm fine, Jeri. Good night. I'll see you tomorrow."

"Good night, Nick. See you tomorrow."

She was gone, the line cutting to static, then to the cold dial tone of the mobile network.

He could only stare as the screen blacked out and locked, just like him.

His existence was blacked out and locked from the rest of the world

He lay on his tiny bed, clutching the phone to his chest, allowing an exhausted sleep to slowly claim him.

But it didn't take too long before he woke up, shaky and disoriented, because there really was no escape from the shadows, where he belonged.

FIVE
THE DANCE

It was a fateful Friday when everything changed. Anticipation hung heavy in the air as the balmy October day slowly gave way to a cool afternoon. He adjusted his red jersey one more time, unable to deny the real weight the Number 4 held for him.

Today was the day. Their first football game of the intercollegiate sports season and Jeri's fateful election for the University Student Council. He took a deep breath and glanced at the clock. It was time to meet his team for the pre-game prep and warm-up. They were last year's regional champions; the expectations this year were quite high.

As he left his room, a cacophony of voices and laughter filled his ears, but his eyes were drawn to one particular sight. There she was, waiting for him just outside the building.

"Hey, how are the elections going?" He closed the distance between them, still unable to understand how she could still think of him with everything else she was doing.

"I...I don't know yet," she stammered, clutching a Tupperware container tightly in her hands. "But I wanted to give you this. I'm sorry I didn't see you this morning. My party-mates and I had to be at the polls extra early to say hello and thank the voters." She hesitated before finally revealing the container's contents: spaghetti.

"Thank you." He took the Tupperware from her hands, noticing how they trembled. It just wasn't her hands. She was pale and her entire body was shaking.

Gently, he took her things and guided her to a nearby bench. "Sit down. You look like you need a minute."

As soon as they were seated, her eyes met his, and she began to cry. The sight of her tears tugged at something inside him, an ache that seemed to mirror her own pain. He wanted to reach out and comfort her, but the words caught in his throat, uncertain what to do with someone in tears. He could kill the cause of her pain, but that wouldn't really help in the long run.

"Do you…do you want to talk about it? Did someone hurt you, or say anything bad?"

Much to his relief, she shook her head. At least that was one less thing he had to worry about.

As her tears flowed, he hesitated for a moment before pulling her into an embrace. Without their usual barriers of bags and books, the sensation of holding her was new yet somewhat familiar; it was as if his arms were designed to cradle her smaller form. Despite her obvious distress, it felt good to hold her.

"Oh, god," she muttered. "You've got a game and here I am ruining you day."

"Don't worry," he said softly, trying to sound as reassuring as possible. "Just tell me what's wrong."

She sniffled, wiping away the tears that stained her cheeks. Her eyes darted around for a moment before they settled on his face.

"I'm scared, Nick. I'm scared shitless of losing, of failing, of being told I'm not good enough. I feel like I have no value if I don't do something meaningful with my life."

The raw honesty of her words cut through him, and he

realized just how much pressure she had been under during this entire campaign. He thought back to all the times he had struggled with his own feelings of inadequacy, with the pressure that he had to be stronger, faster, better than everyone else.

"You mean a lot to so many people, Jeri. You don't have to prove your worth to anyone."

She shook her head, her eyes filling with fresh tears. "I feel like I only have value when people need something from me. That's why I tutor and help others. I want to show everyone that I'm not just...disposable."

Somehow, he felt offended on her behalf. "You're not disposable at all. How could you be, when you mean everything to me?"

Her eyes widened in surprise as his words sunk in, and for a moment, she seemed at a loss for a response. When she finally spoke, her voice trembled with uncertainty.

"Y-you mean you—"

"Yes," he interrupted, pulling her close again, this time without hesitation and awkwardness. "I mean it."

Her arms went around him as her tears soaked into the fabric of his jersey. "You're the only one who really understands, you know. It seems you always know why I need to do what I'm doing. You never question or doubt me. Lexie does, she thinks I'm trying too hard. She worries about me, but I think she's scared of how far and how hard I push myself sometimes. She thinks I might end up hurting myself"

"No," he said firmly. "While I'm here, I won't let that happen."

He knew her best friend tried to understand her, but even Lexie couldn't see past Jeri's relentless drive to succeed. He understood Jeri's need to prove herself, better than anyone else. He'd known it from the start, deep down, the first time he'd seen her speak at the podium during freshman orientation.

"I'll always try to help without asking for anything in return or judging you. Just tell me what to do. I'm yours to command."

Her eyes shimmered with unshed tears as she drew back to look at him. "Why are you so wonderful?"

"It's because of you, Jeri. I don't know what I'm doing half the time, but being with you just feels right. Everything falls into place, as if we're meant to be."

"Meant to be?" she echoed, her eyes searching his. "You mean...together?"

"I don't know," he admitted, shrugging slightly, "but it sure feels that way."

With that, she dove back into his arms. He held on to her quietly for several minutes, memorizing her breathing pattern, the heat of her body against his, and the warm, fruity scent of her skin and hair.

Leaning down, he dared to press a kiss to her forehead. "Let's have dinner together tonight. We can talk more then. I've got my stipend, so we can afford a full spread at one of the eateries across the road."

She giggled through the remainder of her tears, her hands warm as she squeezed his cheeks gratefully. "If I win, it will be my treat, but there's the annual mixer party tonight, remember? If you're coming, we'll see each other there. But make sure you eat first, okay?"

"Sounds perfect," he agreed, taking the container of spaghetti she had prepared for him. "Will you be at my game?"

"Front row," she promised, hugging him quickly before she jumped back to her feet. "Cheering the loudest for you."

He watched her walk away and gave her a wave before she disappeared around the corner of the main building. He crossed the quad and made his way to the classroom next to the field where his team had gathered to prepare for the big game.

The buzz of excitement and tension filled the room. His teammates immediately noticed the Tupperware Jeri had prepared for him, now a familiar sight; their teasing was good-natured and light-hearted.

"Hey Aragon, we're jealous," remarked a senior. "You've got a sweet girlfriend who's probably going to win the election, too. How does it feel to be The Man?"

A freshman chimed in, too, shyly, his eyes wide with admiration. "You've got everything, don't you, Aragon? We can only wish to have half of what you've got."

Before he could respond, their coach walked in, tablet in hand, and began outlining plays and strategies for the game against the maritime college down the road. They were rumored to have strong players this season, but some of those players carried an arrogance from being high school superstars.

After the meeting, they moved to the field to warm up with stretches and team drills. Before he put his phone away next to the makeshift bench at the end of the field, he gave Jeri a quick call to check if the results of the elections had been announced.

Her voice was still shaky from the earlier tension but much calmer. "No, not yet. One of my poll watchers told me I was leading the count about fifteen minutes ago. I'm sure the counting will be over by the time your game finishes."

"Can't wait." He could feel his chest expand, as if there was a balloon of emotion inside him. "Good luck."

"Thanks. Good luck to you, too." She hesitated, then added, "I'll be on the bleachers watching you play. I just wanted to say..." Her voice trailed off, and he heard her take a deep breath. "Never mind. I'll see you later."

"See you." He wanted to know what it was she was trying to say, but now wasn't the time. He put his phone away and joined his teammates on the field, his eyes scanning the bleachers for her face as the number of spectators grew.

The game started shortly, the roar of the crowd filling the campus as he took his position on the field.

He surveyed the opposing team. To their credit, it was a formidable, meticulously assembled line-up, far better than last year's. They had taller, bulkier players; it was an obvious attempt to stuff the roster with people who were physically strong and had a longer reach, similar to him.

As the first half of the game unfolded, he found himself relentlessly pursued by the opposing team's defenders. He could sense their frustration growing with every missed opportunity to stop him. They could fill their ranks however they chose, but they would always have to contend with his real training.

With a few minutes left in the first half, he saw his chance. The ball landed at his feet in a deftly executed pass from his team's vice-captain.

He wove through the opposition like a shadow slipping through cracks of light, the ball seemingly under his complete thrall. Time seemed to slow as he closed in on the goal, his focus narrowing until all he could see was the steel contraption and the grimy white net it held. He planted one foot, drew back the other, and unleashed a strike that sent the ball hurtling into the net.

Goal.

The crowd erupted into deafening cheers that shook the ground. As he jogged past the bleachers, his eyes locked onto Jeri's face amid the sea of spectators. In that moment, it was as if they were the only two people in the world. He waved to her and she waved back, her face splitting into a bright smile.

The second half of the game proved even more intense than the first. The opposing team held nothing back, their defenders swarming around him with more deliberate attempts to keep him away from the goal. They tried to injure him, several times, but he deftly evaded their attacks, as simple as countering deadlier assaults with firearms and blades.

He could feel Jeri's eyes on him, as sure as he could remember her asking if he thought they were meant to be together. As he took position for what could be the decisive goal, he thought of his real answer, and with a surge of determination, he launched the ball towards the right of the net, just a few inches out of the goalie's reach.

No one could stop him.

It was a goal.

The bleachers exploded in wild celebration. He was surrounded by his teammates, coaches, teachers, and classmates, all of them caught up in the euphoria of victory.

The roar in the field had barely subsided when another round of cheers broke out, this time originating from somewhere near the school auditorium.

"Castelo won!" someone shouted, their voice carrying above the din. "She got the most votes out of all the candidates!"

It seemed that today was a day of victories for both of them. Excusing himself from the merriment, he stepped away from the throng of people and retrieved his phone from the bench to call her. To his disappointment, she didn't pick up. Perhaps she was already caught up in her own celebrations.

In the aftermath of the game, the team gathered for an enthusiastic debrief, discussing their plans for winning the regionals once more and defending their title. After the meeting concluded, he retreated to his room, his phone still clutched tightly in his hand. He hesitated, wondering if he should call her again. He didn't want to impose on her well-deserved victory.

Before he could decide what to do next, his phone rang, displaying the name and number of the team's vice-captain, Arthur Posada.

"Hey, Posada."

"Hey, just calling to remind you to come to the college's mixer party tonight, Aragon. It's important we show our solidarity, and the administration will be there. You know how they like to see scholars putting in an appearance. Besides, they all want to see you."

He'd already decided to attend the party, but a reminder of his obligations to keep up appearances was the reality check he needed. He thanked the vice-captain and got ready for the night, dressing in his cleanest, newest blue polo shirt and jeans.

The college mixer was already in full swing at the auditorium by the time he arrived, feeling slightly out of place amid groups of chattering students and loud, thumping music. He wasn't one for social events and tried to avoid them as much as he could.

As he joined his teammates, he was met by an approving nod from his coach and the warm smile of the college dean.

"Congratulations, Aragon," the dean said, shaking his hand firmly. "You've earned that scholarship. Everyone here is proud of your achievements for the university."

"Thank you, sir. It's my honor."

"How is your family taking this? With you so far away but doing such great things for our school?" The look on the dean's face was equal parts sympathy and understanding.

"They are very proud, sir. My brothers can't wait to see me again so we can train together."

"That sounds like good fun," said the dean, clapping him on the back. "Enjoy tonight's party, Aragon. My old bones can only stay until ten, but you kids have fun the rest of the night. Make sure to keep it clean. We don't want the police digging around in the morning."

The dean excused himself and made his way to a group of teachers across the room.

He glanced over at his teammates, who were already enjoying food and soft drinks from the catering tables. He watched as a group of girls and other admirers descended upon them, asking the players to dance or engage in conversation.

Never comfortable with such attention, he quietly backed away from the crowd and, as always, inched into the shadows.

He surveyed the sea of people before him, as the flashing lights installed around the auditorium dipped and swung about in time with the music.

Where was she?

He was so caught up in his thoughts he never noticed the

person who walked up to him and tapped his shoulder lightly. He turned around to see Jeri standing before him, her eyes bright, her cheeks flushed even in the dim light.

"Hey, Aragon," she said playfully, yet her voice wavered ever so slightly. "If you don't dance with me, I will kill you."

His breath caught in his throat at her words, surprised by the uncharacteristic boldness in them and the sudden rush of desire he felt towards her.

She had on a dress with green and white stripes that brought out the smoothness and pinkish tinge of her skin. With her hair arranged in loose waves around her face, she looked breathtakingly luminous, almost untouchable in her beauty.

"Alright, Castelo," he finally replied, trying to sound casual. "No need to threaten me with violence. I'll dance with you."

He hadn't really danced before, but he didn't care.

She didn't say anything when he took her hand. As they moved onto the dance floor in the middle of the auditorium, a slow ballad began to play. He put his hands on her waist; in response, she rested her hands lightly on his shoulders.

"Congratulations," he said as they began swaying to the music. "Heard your victory was a landslide."

She smiled up at him, the pride in her eyes unmistakable. "Thanks. Couldn't have done it without you."

His arms tightened around her, drawing her closer. He wondered if she noticed.

"Congratulations, too," she continued. "You had such a great game. No one could stop you out there. It was amazing to watch. I'm sure you'll go all the way to the championships again."

"Thanks," he replied, pulling her even closer until she was almost completely pressed against him. He wondered if she could feel the raging reaction of his body from being so close to hers. "Is this okay?"

She let out a nervous laugh but bobbed her head gently. "Is

it just me or do I feel like we've done this before?"

"Maybe in another life," he answered, his lips brushing her hair.

She sighed and closed the last few inches that separated them, her arms coiling around his neck, as high and as tightly as her height would allow.

"What about this life?" she muttered against his chest. The warmth of her breath through the thin fabric of his shirt felt undeniably intimate.

"You tell me, Jeri."

"I don't know. Her cheek settled comfortably on the spot where his heart was. "But I don't want this to end."

She had no idea how much he'd wanted to say the exact same thing to her.

I wish my time with you would never end.

But the song was over, leaving him breathless and unsure of what to do next.

She stepped back, avoiding eye contact. He averted his eyes, too. Acknowledging the intensity of the moment might make it too real—once he crossed that line, there would be no turning back.

"Nick, can we talk about what just happened?" Her hand found his in the darkness. Her touch was cold and slightly damp. He knew his reaction was almost the same.

"Of course." It was all he could say.

She led him to a secluded corner at the backstage area of the auditorium, past layers upon layers of dusty dark red stage curtains, their way illuminated by a few old lightbulbs. Away from the crowd, they found themselves alone in what looked like a broken-down dressing room. There were two chairs in front of the cracked mirror. As if in silent agreement, they both stayed on their feet. She still clung to his hand, a little too tightly.

"I feel like I've taken advantage of our friendship and your kindness," she began hesitantly. "You've always been so nice to me and I feel like I've insulted you. I'm really sorry. I think I got carried away. Today has been particularly overwhelming."

Her voice was barely audible over the distant hum of the ongoing party, but he could see the uncertainty and fear in her eyes in the semi-darkness.

What was she so afraid of?

He reached for her other hand, this time intertwining his fingers with hers. He brought her hands up to his chin, as if keeping them next to his skin would warm her up.

"You don't have to apologize. We danced. That was all, wasn't it?"

She shook her head. "Was it only a dance to you? I don't even know how to act around you anymore. I don't know what I feel for you. I don't even know what we have between us. It fucks with my head so badly."

Before she could say anything more, he leaned in and captured her lips in a kiss.

It was his first kiss.

And he let go.

It was passionate and intense. Again and again, their lips met, each kiss increasing in urgency with which he craved her touch, her taste.

"Is this the real you?" she whispered when they finally pulled apart, her breath ragged and her eyes wide with wonder.

"Yes," he responded without hesitation. "It is, only with you."

He didn't say anything more as his hands moved to the straps of her dress, his fingertips brushing the softness of her skin as he slowly lowered the fabric to reveal more of her. He marveled at the curves and delicate lines of her body, everything that made her so perfect in his eyes.

"Nick, I..." she began to protest, stopping his hands in their path. "You know I'm not..." Her voice trailed off as she glanced down at herself.

"You're the most beautiful girl in the world to me, Jeri."

Tenderly, he explored her with his mouth. He started with her neck and chest, his tongue tracing circles around the taut nipples once her ample, perfectly round breasts found their way out of her bra. He settled her on the old dresser and kissed her lips before his fingers continued their journey downward.

"Trust me, you are perfect just as you are," he assured her, as he parted her legs, his hands tracing the curve of her hips before sliding her panties off.

He lifted the skirt of her dress and kissed his way from her knees upward, his tongue leaving a damp path along the way. His lips traced the curves of her inner thighs, inches away from the very heart of her that radiated white-hot heat. The scent of her engulfed him like an irresistibly intoxicating cloud; it was so uniquely her it was all he could do not to bury himself inside her.

He took a deep breath and pressed his lips to her core, his tongue joyously lapping up the taste of her as she moaned and writhed on the dresser, her partially exposed breasts bouncing, her legs parting wider to make way for more of the sensations he was giving her.

"Nick," she panted, her hips grinding against his mouth. Her hands dug into his shoulders and pulled at his hair in turn as her movements increased in urgency. Jeri losing control against a broken dressing room mirror was the most incredibly erotic sight he had ever laid eyes on.

It took one more suckle at her nub and one more deep stroke of his fingers before she let out a loud moan, finally getting to the peak he so desperately wanted her to reach.

Her body stiffened, then abruptly went limp in the aftermath of her climax. He caught her in his arms as she wavered from her seated position. He held her close, listening to her rapid heartbeat, their breaths mingling together as the lingering scent of her engulfed his senses.

He savored the sensation of her legs wrapped loosely around

his hips, her arms draped over his shoulders, her damp hair plastered all over her face and his. This was the most intimate he had ever been with anyone.

He was the first to speak, his lips against her ear as he inhaled her now-familiar cologne, mingled with her sweat, from the throbbing pulse on her neck. "I've never been with someone before. I've never even kissed anyone. You're the first."

"Me, too," she breathed. "You're my first kiss…the first boy who's ever touched me. You're my first everything."

She pulled him close, kissing his cheek and burying her nose in his hair. It was a strange, yet deeply moving, gesture.

"I've never had a boyfriend before," she continued. "I've always been so focused on my studies, on helping others, on being a student leader. I never had time for…love. Definitely not this kind."

"Until now?" He felt something akin to hope stir in his chest.

"Until now," she confirmed, almost shyly.

Their lips met again, tenderly at first, then more urgently, hungrily. His hands found her exposed breasts once more, but before he could reach for the damp spot between her legs again, her hands slid into his shirt.

She hesitated briefly before going lower, her fingers finally daring to reach inside his jeans. "Is this okay?"

"Y-yes," he stuttered as his body coiled in anticipation.

She reached into his underwear and took him in her hand. He gasped and cursed under his breath, gritting his teeth.

Encouraged, she continued, rubbing and stroking him. He didn't know he could get any harder, but he did. He was almost at breaking point.

She slid off the dresser, straightening her clothes as she went, and pushed him against the wall. He was achingly aware she still wasn't wearing her panties; they were somewhere in a damp ball on one of the nearby chairs.

She went down on her knees and undid his zipper, pushing his underwear down just enough to free his rock-hard arousal. He groaned when she bent her head and took him into her mouth, her lips moving up and down his length in a maddening rhythm.

He felt an electric current shoot through him, and his entire body tensed as he climaxed right in her mouth. The waves of pleasure that coursed through his body were so strong they threatened to tear him apart. Her name escaped his lips in a raw, guttural moan, rumbling in his chest and through the dusty air of the backstage area.

She stood up and put her arms around his waist, as if to hold him upright.

"You're amazing," he whispered into her hair.

"So are you," she replied.

They kissed once more, tongues tangling, tasting each other with a newfound sense of closeness. He hardened again, almost immediately; this time, there was no hiding it from her.

"Jeri, what are we supposed to do now?"

"I don't know," she admitted, her fingers gripping his rumpled shirt tightly. "But I don't want us to end, whatever this is we've got."

I don't want us to end, he echoed inwardly.

They were an *'us'* now.

It was all he'd ever wanted.

Everything he'd ever needed, since the first time he saw her.

"Whatever you want to do, I'm here for you. I'll follow you anywhere."

"Would you?"

He nodded.

He felt, more than he saw, her smile.

He smiled back as his hand found hers in the shadows.

From then on, he never let go.

ACT 2
Fallen

SIX

THE DESIRE

He had her in his arms, for now.

As he held her, he still marveled at how they both appeared to be so different from each other.

She was the epitome of intelligence and charisma. Everyone liked her—from the teachers, to the cafeteria staff, most if not all of the student body. She always had that ready smile and the time to listen to everyone's problems.

People believed that sleeping wasn't on her busy schedule, the same way she believed he didn't sleep at all.

Everyone knew that Jeri Castelo would rather stay up talking to someone in her trademark high-octane and witty manner, organizing events as a member of the University Student Council for the second year in a row, or tutoring other students in Calculus.

He was popular in another fashion: the star football player who never gave away much about himself.

The name Aragon struck fear in the football teams of colleges all over the region. Ever since his freshman year, he had brought the university an unprecedented steady stream of championships.

He was not, however, raised to become an athletic achiever. His training had aimed to accomplish more serious ends.

Deadly serious ends.

In his first year, their class had gone on a trip up the mountains as part of their Biology subject. While everyone had lugged bags of canned goods and other packaged foods, he had only brought clothes and minimal camping equipment.

Evening at their campsite, the teacher had asked, "Where's the dinner you're supposed to bring for yourself?"

"It's right behind you, sir." He had thrown his hunting knife, the blade whizzing a mere inch above his professor's head.

A wild chicken, an *ilahas*, had squawked and crashed to the ground in rapid succession.

He then had an entire roasted chicken for his dinner, served hot. No one shared his meal, or spoke to him for the rest of the trip. The teacher gave him a grade of 1.0.

After that, everyone dealt with him very cautiously. No one dared to test his temper, even though he had never once displayed it, on or off the field.

He'd liked things that way, or so he thought. The further he distanced himself, the better.

Only Jeri had dared break through the wall between him and the rest of the world.

Ever since that fateful night more than a year ago, he knew he had fallen in love with her, more and more deeply with each passing day.

She had not been of any help, either. She had wanted and loved him, too.

At the end of the evening they first danced and kissed, they had made love, nervously and tenderly, on his tiny bed in the main building's basement.

He had never imagined he would feel that way, when his body, lean and hardened by years of training, was intertwined with hers, soft and welcoming.

He remembered the first time he'd touched her hair, the first time he'd allowed himself to look into her eyes without any qualms, the first time he'd kissed her as much as he wanted to.

He remembered the first time she'd allowed him to take off her clothes and taste all of her.

It was only later, in the aftermath of their passionate encounter, did he figure out that she'd reminded him of apples.

Since then, he had been unable to distance himself or stop thinking about her, no matter how hard he'd tried to deny how he really felt.

Ever since their freshman year, the distance between him and the perfection that was Jeri Castelo had seemed impossible to bridge.

She shone as brightly and as purely as the sun, on a day without clouds.

He was only a shadow, a dreary mass of dark secrets.

But, for now, he felt whole, from her touch and her light.

Now was all he ever had with her, he thought, as his reverie of their time together melted away, bringing him back into the present, with her in his bed, wrapped in his arms.

Jeri peeled off his shirt, her fingers brushing over the eagle tattoo etched over his heart. He felt her hands run over his shoulders and his stomach. With a moan, she moved closer, climbing onto his lap and wrapping her legs around his waist as they continued to kiss each other.

He reached up and began to unbutton her blouse, slowly revealing her delicate skin. His eyes drank in the sight of her, his heart racing with the familiar combination of desire and fear, as if he was seeing her for the first time all over again. He unclasped her bra and gently traced his fingers along her curves before lowering his mouth to her nipples, licking and biting them softly, making her gasp.

He continued to explore her body, his fingers deftly unzipping her skirt and slipping it off along with her panties until she was completely naked before him. Her pinkish skin was flushed under the lights.

He focused on her inner thighs, coaxing her to open for him, his body humming with excitement as she gave in so willingly and sweetly to his unspoken request. As his mouth descended upon her, she cried his name out, her hands pulling at his hair.

"Please don't stop, Nick." Her voice was barely audible above the pounding of his own heart, as his arousal tried to fight its way out of the confines of his clothes.

But he was going to take his time. Patience was something he was very good at.

He began tentatively, by tasting her, his tongue tracing intricate patterns across her sensitive flesh. His fingers soon joined the fray as he brought her to the peak, a hoarse scream coming from her throat.

He held her close as she slowly came down from the heights of her pleasure. He kissed her hair and her cheeks as she trembled in his arms, panting as if she had run around the campus herself.

He didn't have to wait very long for her to catch her breath.

She reached for the waistband of his joggers, slowly lowering them to reveal his hardness.

His gaze never left hers as he gently positioned himself between her legs. He took a moment to make sure she was wet, using his length to tease her entrance. The sensation of her slick folds against him always drove him to the very edge, no matter how many times he had her.

"Fuck, you feel so good."

She cupped his cheeks and kissed him soundly on the lips. "So do you."

With those words, she put her arms around his shoulders and her legs around his hips.

He allowed himself to sink deep into her. He wrapped his arms around her tightly as he began to thrust into her, slowly, languidly.

They began to move together in a sensual rhythm. He could feel the tension building within him, the heat and pressure coiling tighter and tighter as he lost himself in her embrace.

"I can't hold back," he gasped out as he teetered on the brink.

"Let go," she urged him softly. "I'm here with you. I love you."

With the warmth and tenderness of her reassurance enveloping him, he lost control, surrendering to the tidal wave of pleasure that crashed over him.

"I love you, too," he heard himself say. "Now come for me."

As he thrust into her in the final throes of his own climax, he heard her cry out his name as she, too, gave her surrender.

For now, she was with him, as close as two people could possibly be.

For now, her light was his, too.

SEVEN
THE DREAM

Was this a dream?

His heart pounded as he gazed at the woman in his arms, their bodies tangled together on his narrow bed. His fingertips traced lazy patterns on her skin, marveling at the warmth of her that seemed to surround him completely.

When he finally found his voice, her name sounded like a desperate plea.

"Jeri."

She looked into his eyes, her own gaze reflecting his desire, before she cupped his cheek and leaned in to kiss him deeply. Their tongues danced together, exploring each other's mouths.

"Yes," she murmured between kisses. "Always yes."

With renewed vigor, he rolled them over, positioning himself above her once more. This time, she spread her legs wide, raising her hips to meet his mid-air. He slid his hands under her buttocks to lift her slightly, and then filled her in one quick surge.

He reveled in the sensation of her body fitting so perfectly against his, in the way she responded to his touch—and he to hers. He came with a thunderous roar, as she shook under him, her hair spreading all over his pillow as her breasts bounced enticingly with each of thrust.

It wasn't too long before he took her again, this time from behind, his hands gripping her hips tightly before moving to cup her breasts and caress her nipples.

After they recovered, he held her in his lap, their faces close as if sharing the same breath, as they exchanged tender kisses while they made love once more.

He didn't care if this was all only a dream.

It was a heady blend of tender emotion and fiery passion. He knew he would never tire of the feel of her body against his, the way her moans and sighs echoed in his ears, the softness of her arms around him.

He was completely and utterly lost in her.

Momentarily sated, they lay quietly in each other's arms.

"You should eat more," she declared out of the blue. "I need to bring you more food."

"Really?"

"Yes. I don't know where you get all that energy to move so fast, or kick that hard. Or to run so much every day." Her breath tickled the bare skin of his chest. "Or to do *this*."

"I don't know. Habit, maybe."

They both lapsed into silence.

She reached for his hands. He felt her delicate skin brush against his scarred and callused palms.

"It must be time for practice soon," she finally said.

He found his phone in the pocket of his discarded joggers. The display told him they still had a little more than an hour left before he had to go to the field.

He turned to look at her, naked in his bed, his blanket wrapped around her for modesty. "Would you like some breakfast?"

She nodded. "I'm starving."

He put his phone away and joined her, reaching for her underneath the blanket.

"Me, too."

As he took her back into his arms and kissed her again, he hoped he could stay in the dream long enough.

EIGHT
THE DECEPTION

The sky was still a deep, murky grey when they walked out of the main building. Morning, classes, and the rest of the world would be upon them soon.

She paused when they reached the middle of the quad, her eyes settling on the grassy field in front of them.

"The first time I saw you, you were practicing alone," she said softly. "It was the first day of freshman year. It was Orientation Week and I came in early. I wanted to introduce myself to people as they arrived. I saw you on the field when I walked up to this spot, right here."

He swallowed hard as he absorbed the weight of her words, the depth of the memory she now shared. All he could do was take her hand and listen.

"It was like watching something both magnificent and deadly at the same time. It was raining, but you never even missed a shot. The way you moved, the way you stood there, on your own, defying the downpour...you didn't seem to care. You were just so focused and determined. But I never approached you because I thought...well, I thought you'd only be interested in tall, pretty girls, like the ones football players and jocks usually go for."

He felt a chuckle rumble through his chest.

Very few people had seen him smile. But she was the only one who heard him laugh.

She elbowed him in the ribs "What the hell's so funny?"

"You." He pulled her close as they looked at the field still blanketed by darkness. "Why do you always have to be so fucking *perfect*? You remember, know, and do almost everything."

Her breathing seemed to stop. It took moments before she could answer. "I was raised to be like that. No one could make up for my mistakes, if I was stupid enough to make them. When I moved in with my grandparents after my parents died, I learned this very quickly."

She paused, as if gathering momentum. "When I was little, my grandmother would slap my hands with a stick whenever I couldn't spell a word correctly. Or, sometimes, they wouldn't let me have dinner unless I could recite an entire speech without any mistakes. I got good at all of it. Then better. By the time I was eight, there was no more need for such discipline. I delivered everything they wanted."

"When I got older, my grandparents told me my mother failed them by eloping with my father. She had me when she was eighteen. And I…I couldn't fail my family."

The words had a pained, bitter edge. He could taste them in his own heart. If there was someone who understood, only too well, how it was like to rise to the nearly impossible expectations and demands of their family, it was him.

"It gets exhausting. I'm doing a great job at it, though. There are so many people expecting so many things. I had to do all those things. I feel guilty when I couldn't. Sometimes it's like digging your own grave. But you need to do it anyway." Her voice sounded rough and strained. "Being perfect was the only way to survive, to keep having value."

The first few raindrops fell. He felt them on his arm. Then

he realized they weren't from the sky. The droplets were her tears.

Something bubbled inside him. It wasn't rage, but a calmer desire to kill. It was part of him, his lifeblood.

Although he had vowed to himself never to take a human life again, he would break that for her, to spare her from any further pain.

But there was no one entirely responsible for the sort of torment she felt. Just like no one had to pay for his past and the choices he'd made, except perhaps he himself.

"I'm sorry…" His voice trailed off. He felt lame and helpless, as the familiar cold numbness ran the length of his spine. It was a feeling only pulling the trigger could relieve. "I shouldn't have said–"

"It's not your fault. Sometimes I just couldn't help but think about this, no matter how hard I try not to." She bravely swallowed back her sobs as he wiped her tears away. "I had it coming. I had it coming all these years. It was only a matter of time before I got burned out."

He waited for her to calm down. She could so easily collect herself, or at least appear to have done so. He was the only one who would always know and feel the trembling of her hands, the uneven beating of her pulse, even if she appeared perfectly composed.

She had looked like this during debates when she ran for the University Student Council a second time, when after she'd felt like ice to his touch. Everyone else had praised her composure and quick thinking, never considering the amount of control it took on her part.

With all the light she radiated, she still had the cold, dark parts, too.

NINE
THE DEAL

"I was raised to be the best, too," he admitted, slowly, cautiously. "I became the best."

Jeri's tearstained face had a look that showed the struggle to comprehend his words. She said nothing, but spoke volumes with wide eyes.

He knew at that point he had to explain, to make her understand.

There was no turning back now, not after everything they had shared.

"When I was in high school, I was known as Cain in the underground. My father chose that name for me. I was born with a twin brother, but my cord was around his neck when we were cut out…I choked him to death in our mother's womb."

"I didn't know…" She was grasping at words. "You never—"

He squeezed her hands in his, shaking his head slightly.

It was his way of telling her it was okay. He would be okay, if he had her with him.

"I'm the youngest of five brothers, but I could outshoot all of them. I could take them all down hand to hand, too, by the time I was seven. I was faster and stronger. I was even better in most sports. A lot of schools offered everything from bribes to scholarship packages to my parents so I would go to their place, just so they could get all the football titles, even a National Games medal."

"My father told us that the mantle of the Eagle-Eye had to be passed down. He was almost sixty and it was about time for him to mentor the next one. All my uncles—everyone in my family—wanted me to take it. I was fourteen. The Eagle-Eye tattoo meant the world."

"That explains the eagle mark on your chest." Jeri placed her hand over his heart. "It's more than just a tattoo."

"Our family has been in the Philippines for more than three hundred years. You can say we wrote a lot of history in blood and no one ever knew. We are loyal to no one, except our own kin and land. That's how we had roots. The Eagle-Eye is the best of the present generation. He was entrusted to carry out the most dangerous missions."

He said everything without any pride. Then again, there was nothing to be proud of.

A series of frozen frames flashed in his memory. He drew in a sharp breath at how vividly he could remember the events of seven years past.

"My initiation rite was to kill a priest who had sexually abused the son of one of our workers at the corn farm. The boy was eight, a *sacristan*. It was three-thirty in the morning…the priest was walking to Church to prepare for the *misa de gallo*. I got him with one shot, right between the eyes. It was Christmas—and my fifteenth birthday—when I became the ninth-generation Eagle-Eye. That's when I got the tattoo. Then my father said, 'You will be Cain now.'"

"There are twenty-nine others on my list; two of them were very young, maybe seven or eight years old. They were the children of a drug lord who thought he could smuggle *shabu* through one of the canning companies in our town. They saw me shoot their father. *Leave no witnesses.* That was in the rules."

"You killed people." Her voice was toneless. Not angry, afraid or accusing, just clear and audible.

"I left Surallah thinking I could somehow lose that part of me. I bargained for four years to finish college so there's time to think about it. No matter how hard you try, that side of you stays right where it is. If you try to get rid of it somehow, it will eat you up alive. You could shed your skin, but not your blood. You wouldn't have the strength to survive."

He realized she had not backed away, or showed any sign of fear or disgust.

Before he could say anything more, she looked straight into his eyes, unblinking. He could see the clarity in her gaze, behind the sheen of tears, in the soft light of the oncoming sunrise.

"I love you, Nick. Nothing's going to change that."

TEN

THE DAWN

Nick.

He was only ever Aragon to everyone else.

To Jeri, he'd always been her Nick.

The absence of revulsion from her took him aback. "I know I should have told you before. I couldn't, Jeri. I didn't want to lose you. I'm so sorry—"

"There's nothing to be sorry for." Her tone was firm, although she spoke in a voice so quiet it was almost carried away by the early morning breeze. "I loved you for what you are. I found in you a part of myself I thought I'd never find in anyone else."

He swallowed hard, ice and dread gripping his insides. "You're not angry, are you?"

She shook her head. "Why should I be? Because you told me the truth?"

"But I'm a…*killer.* You should be walking away right now."

Jeri did the exact opposite.

She put her arms around him. "I'm staying right here. I'm not going anywhere. Don't you know how good it feels to finally hear you talk about where you came from?"

"Jeri, I…" His voice trailed off. He had no words for her. He only had himself and everything else. He'd lay them all at her feet in a heartbeat.

She took his hand and placed it gently on her belly. "I love you for being the father of this child."

It took him a second to understand what she meant by both her actions and words. When he finally did, he felt all the air leave his lungs.

He could only stare at her as a sudden glow began to form in the pit of his stomach. It was the familiar warmth he had known only when he met her.

When he finally mustered some semblance of self-control, he said, "Are you…?"

He couldn't finish the question. The idea was too unreal, too beautiful, to speak of. Part of him feared it would disappear right before his eyes, along with her.

Instead, she smiled brightly. "Maybe six weeks now. A doctor who doesn't know my family confirmed it yesterday afternoon. That's why I had to see you. I could no longer keep this a secret." Her face, so breathtakingly beautiful to him, was a study in mixed emotions. "I had to tell you."

"I'm going to be a father," he said slowly, tasting the word. He put his hands on her stomach, over her own. His own blood, now with hers.

Father, he repeated inwardly. A father.

She nodded.

This time, the first real drops of rain started to fall.

A droplet landed on his lips. He tasted sweetness and warmth. It bore none of the bitter taste and spilled blood of the past three hundred years.

A bolt of lightning streaked across the sky, followed by a loud rumble of thunder, just before the rain came down in earnest.

In silent agreement, neither of them suggested taking shelter in the nearby gazebos surrounding the campus quad.

Jeri stepped back and spread out her arms, giggling as she turned her face up to the downpour.

As he watched her spinning slowly under the rain, he realized that he was still half-stunned by her news.

She paused for a moment, her movements punctuated by a soft giggle. "Nick, I want to dance with you."

In that moment, his head cleared, as if someone had shone a light on the shadows of his burden. He took her hands in his and placed her palms over his heart, on the very same spot where his body bore the Eagle-Eye mark. "I love you."

She smiled and stood on tiptoe, pressing her lips to his. "For the first time in our lives, let's not be the best assassin or the perfect girl. Let's do the right thing and just be us."

He nodded. "Us," he repeated, trying the sound of the word rolling off his tongue.

He'd always liked the ring of it, remembering the first time she had used the word to describe what they had.

I don't want us to end.

The rain fell harder.

He basked in the sight of the woman who had looked him in the eye and never wavered, even after his confession and the deaths he had brought.

Instead, she embraced him and his blood.

She looked straight back at him, the same way she had the night of their first dance. The night she'd opened the door to his heart and, unwittingly, to his freedom from the shadows of the past.

Nicholas Aragon embraced her then.

Nothing more was said.

The rain crashed around them, drenching concrete, earth, steel, and their bodies.

When the sun finally rose, the thunderstorm came to an end. Only the wind was left howling, singing a dirge to the shadows as they became one with the light.

EPILOGUE
THE LAST LETTER

It was Lexie's habit, for the past two years now, to drop by the newspaper office every morning to check on messages and writing assignments.

When she arrived, on the dot, at half-past seven, the first thing she noticed was a folded note tacked to the corkboard. Her name was on it, in a familiar roundish script.

She took the paper off the board and unlocked the door.

The note felt slightly damp in her hands as she unfolded it. The paper seemed to have gotten wet in the heavy rain earlier that morning and was slowly drying out.

My dearest Lexie,

I've held on for years to what I thought I was.

I have become the perfect puppet to expectations that were never mine. It's time to cut the strings.

I gave them my entire life, until now. From today, it's my turn to live the rest of it on my own terms.

I will miss you.

Love always,

Jeri

She stared at the signature. Like her best friend's personality, it had an undeniable, inimitable flourish.

For a long time, Lexie stood in the middle of the empty office, her gaze seeing beyond the unlit space before her.

She went through the drafts left on the table for her to review, locked up, and headed to her first class of the day.

Along the way, she stopped by one of the trash cans on the quad and tore the letter to shreds. She watched the tiny white pieces fall from her hands like raindrops disappearing into the cold morning air.

"Be happy, Jeri," she whispered. "I'll miss you, too."

About the Author

Shirley Siaton writes edgy and evocative stories and poems. Her worlds are in a deliciously dark cross-section of the romance, neo-noir, action, fantasy, new adult and contemporary genres.

She has several books of fiction and poetry released since February 2023. Her first book is the free verse collection *Black Cat and other poems*. She also pens juvenile literature as Shirley Parabia.

She is an award-winning writer, poet and journalist in English, Filipino and Hiligaynon, lauded by the Stevan Javellana Foundation, Philippine Information Agency and West Visayas State University. Her essays, short stories and poems have been published internationally in print and digital media. Her multi-lingual plays have been staged in the Philippines.

Shirley is a black belt in Shotokan Karate and an international certified fitness coach. Originally from Iloilo City, she is based in the Middle East with her husband and two daughters.

Links

Shirley's official website:
shirleysiaton.com

Complete reading guide:
shirley.pub

Subscribe to Shirley's VIP list for free exclusive updates:
newsletter.shirleysiaton.com

www.ingramcontent.com/pod-product-compliance
Lightning Source LLC
LaVergne TN
LVHW041515170726
843492LV00005B/1515

AF454296

DESSINS ET MODÈLES

—

LA SCULPTURE DÉCORATIVE

4° V 3259 (5)

ALBUMS FORMANT LA COLLECTION

DES

DESSINS ET MODÈLES

Album des Arts du bois........ 164 gravures.
   — des Arts du feu......... 223   —
   — des Arts du métal....... 200   —
   — des Arts du tissu....... 150   —
   — de Peinture décorative... 200   —
   — de Sculpture décorative.. 166   —

BORDEAUX. — IMPR. G. GOUNOUILHOU, RUE GUIRAUDE, 11.
PARIS. — RUE DE RICHELIEU, 101.

DESSINS ET MODÈLES

LA

SCULPTURE DÉCORATIVE

(Statues — Groupes — Bas-Reliefs)

NOTICE par M. Louis BAUZON

Album comprenant 166 Gravures

PARIS

BIBLIOTHÈQUE DE LA *GAZETTE DES BEAUX-ARTS*

J. ROUAM & Cie, éditeurs

14, RUE DU HELDER, 14

NOTICE HISTORIQUE

Il n'est pas aussi facile qu'on peut le croire de donner de la sculpture décorative une définition qui satisfasse tout le monde. Où commence et où finit la sculpture « décorative »? En quoi consiste-t-elle précisément? quel est son rôle? quelles sont les conditions et les règles du genre? Questions multiples, opinions diverses. Mais ce n'est pas ici le lieu d'engager ces discussions théoriques. Il suffira de dire que la sculpture peut être appelée « décorative » quand elle se propose de concourir à l'embellissement d'un monument relevant à un titre quelconque de l'art architectural.

A ce compte, les figures de Phidias au fronton du Parthénon et les taureaux à tête humaine des palais de Khorsabad, les nymphes de Jean Goujon sur la Fontaine des Innocents et les figures sculptées par notre grand Puget à la proue des navires, les statues de pierre au portail de nos cathédrales et les grands anges de bois au couronnement de nos vieux buffets d'orgue rentrent également dans le domaine de la sculpture décorative. Et pourquoi les figures et les ornements, plus modestes, de nos meubles, de nos buffets, de nos crédences, de nos coffres anciens, de nos jubés, de nos chœurs d'églises, de nos chaires, etc., n'en seraient-ils pas aussi?

Feuilletez d'ailleurs l'album ci-joint; tournez-en les pages si intéressantes, si variées, si curieuses; passez en revue tous ces spécimens recueillis de partout, empruntés à toute civilisation et à tout âge, dessinés d'après le marbre ou le bronze, comme d'après le bois ou la pierre, et vous serez édifiés sur la nature, l'étendue, l'intérêt et le charme de la sculpture décorative : cette « leçon de choses » vaudra toutes les définitions, cet abondant recueil de belles images vous en apprendra tout autant que de savants et volumineux traités.

Il serait oiseux de remonter ici aux âges préhistoriques et de se

demander ce que pouvait bien être la sculpture décorative au temps de
l'homme primitif. Disons pourtant que les armes, les ustensiles et les
ornements de la « pierre taillée », premiers essais de l'art naissant,
sont déjà par certains côtés de la sculpture, et que cette sculpture est
« décorative ». C'est ainsi que le premier sauvage qui modela grossiè-
rement en forme de vague figure ses instruments rudimentaires, ou qui
tailla, d'après quelque ressemblance humaine ou animale, les troncs
de bois mal équarris qui soutenaient son toit de chaume ou de roseaux,
fut le précurseur lointain des Phidias et des Jean Goujon.

Mais laissons de côté la question des origines, avec ses problèmes,
ses obscurités, ses mystères, et hâtons-nous d'arriver aux premières
époques historiques, déjà riches en exemples et en documents.

Le voyageur qui explore les ruines antiques découvertes ou exhu-
mées à diverses époques dans la vallée du Nil ou dans celles du Tigre
et de l'Euphrate, ou simplement le curieux qui parcourt, au rez-de-
chaussée du Louvre, les salles réservées à l'Égypte, à la Chaldée et à
l'Assyrie, n'ont pas besoin qu'on leur explique ce qu'était la sculpture
décorative au pays des Pharaons ou des Sargonides : les plus ins-
tructifs et les plus précieux vestiges de la décoration sculpturale telle
que la comprenaient les contemporains de Sémiramis, de Nabucho-
donosor et de Sargon, ou de Thoutmès et de Sésostris, subsistent
merveilleusement conservés souvent, parmi ce qui reste de Ninive
et de Babylone, ou de Thèbes et de Memphis ; des fragments admira-
bles de cet art bien antérieur à celui de la Grèce ornent nos musées :
Khorsabad et Louqsor ont enrichi le Louvre ; Nimroud, Kouioundjik
et Memphis décorent le British Museum.

Les monuments égyptiens se distinguent, au point de vue qui
nous préoccupe, par trois caractères également remarquables : la
sculpture décorative y joue partout un rôle capital, elle s'y présente
très souvent sous la forme colossale, elle s'y trouve unie et mariée à
l'architecture de la façon la plus étroite et la plus intime. — Qu'il
s'agisse d'un édifice civil ou d'un monument religieux, d'un temple
ou d'un palais, ces trois caractères se retrouvent presque toujours
unis. Prenons pour exemple la façade du fameux temple souterrain
d'Abou Simbel, ou Ibsamboul, en Nubie. Quatre statues assises du roi
Ramsès, taillées en plein roc, en pleine montagne, décorent l'entrée
du sanctuaire ; elles ont vingt mètres de haut, elles sont tellement
inhérentes au monument qu'on ne saurait les en détacher par la
pensée : elles sont le monument lui-même. Les grandes figures,
moindres, mais colossales encore, qui semblent s'abriter entre leurs
pieds énormes ; le dieu à tête d'épervier, debout, énigmatique, inquié-

tant, qui surmonte et garde, dans sa niche rectangulaire, la porte de l'édifice; la rangée de vingt-deux singes cynocéphales assis, de deux mètres cinquante de haut, qui couronne cette imposante façade, si étrange et si simple à la fois; les personnages et les animaux, ces lettres-images, des gigantesques hiéroglyphes gravés et modelés sur les surfaces planes, sur les soubassements, sur les frises du prodigieux portail de cette cathédrale égyptiaque, tous ces ornements d'un goût grandiose font corps avec le monument : une saisissante impression d'unité se dégage de l'ensemble.

Presque toutes les surfaces libres, dans ces monuments d'une conception si une, sont couvertes de reliefs méplats et richement colorés, dont les motifs sont empruntés à la symbolique, à l'histoire, à la religion, aux scènes multiples et variées de la vie réelle. Cette décoration, lisons-nous dans Lubke, reproduit « l'histoire ou plutôt la chronique de la vie égyptienne, divisée en chapitres distincts, correspondant à la nature des espaces décorés ». C'est ainsi que chaque monument nouveau devenait, au pays des Pharaons, comme un chapitre de l'histoire nationale : les annales du peuple égyptien se perpétuaient, chez ce peuple soucieux d'éternité, sur les parois indestructibles des palais, des temples, des tombeaux.

Cette continuelle intervention de la statuaire et son intime union avec l'architecture, apparaissent partout, à l'intérieur comme au dehors, dans ce qui nous reste des monuments de l'ancienne Égypte : dans l'immense salle hypostyle de Karnak, par exemple, aussi bien que dans les hypogées d'Ibsamboul, sur les façades de Denderah ou d'Edfou, comme aux salles intérieures du Ramesseum. Partout la sculpture apparaît et s'étale aux échelles et sous les formes les plus diverses, et partout elle concourt à l'unité comme à la beauté de l'ensemble. Tous les autres édifices, dit Viollet-le-Duc, perdent en face de l'art égyptien quelque chose de leur unité : le regard se reporte involontairement vers cette puissante et suprême expression de l'union des trois arts.

On aurait été fort empêché, il y a seulement un demi-siècle, de parler avec quelque précision des arts de l'Assyrie et de la Chaldée; on n'en connaissait presque rien encore que ce qu'avaient pu dire çà et là, d'une façon grandiose et vague, les Livres Saints et les auteurs grecs : l'art de la Mésopotamie est une découverte contemporaine. C'est en 1842 qu'un Français, le consul de Botta, commença les fouilles de Kouioundjik, où fut Ninive, et celles de Khorsabad, où fut Dur Sariukin, la ville de Sargon; c'est en 1846 que l'Anglais Layard, éventrant la colline de Nimroud, exhuma les ruines de Kalak, une capitale inconnue jusque-là; c'est de 1851 à 1853 que les Français

Fresnel et Thomas, accompagnés de l'archéologue Oppert, découvrirent sur les deux rives de l'Euphrate, près du village d'Hillah, les ruines de l'antique Babylone.

Là comme en Égypte, et plus qu'en Égypte encore, les monuments ont des proportions immenses; là comme en Égypte, la sculpture décorative étale ses hauts et ses bas-reliefs sur les parois des monuments. Seulement, dans ces plaines d'alluvions, les matériaux sont rares : les constructions sont faites en briques crues, cimentées de bitume; les sculptures sont modelées sur de grandes et minces plaques de calcaire, de marbre ou d'albâtre. Les sujets favoris des artistes assyriens paraissent avoir été les exploits cynégétiques ou guerriers, les expéditions et les victoires de leurs rois, la vie et les scènes de la cour. Tantôt cette sculpture officielle nous montre, comme dans la riche collection du Musée Britannique, Sennachérib en expédition, debout sur son char, suivi de ses officiers, de ses serviteurs et de ses gardes, ou Assurbanipal en chasse, tirant de l'arc, au galop de son cheval, sur les bêtes qui fuient. Tantôt, comme au Louvre, elle nous représente Sargon et son cortège royal, son grand-vizir, ses officiers de cour, ses porteurs d'emblèmes, de sièges, de vases et d'ustensiles de toutes sortes, s'avançant en longue file, solennels et dignes.

Les meilleures de ces sculptures sont remarquables par la fermeté du dessin, la saisissante netteté des silhouettes, la précision et la finesse du travail. Les artistes assyriens, plus libres probablement dans la représentation des animaux que dans celle des hommes, ont surtout laissé d'admirables études de chevaux, de lions, de taureaux, de chiens, etc., chefs-d'œuvre d'observation et de style, traités dans une manière large et précise qu'on n'a point surpassée : la fameuse lionne blessée du Musée Britannique, percée de flèches, qui se relève, en rugissant, sur ses pattes de devant, tandis que le reste de son corps, déjà paralysé, traîne inerte et raidi, a tout le caractère et toute la simplicité grandiose d'un Barye.

Ce furent souvent aussi des artistes à l'imagination originale et féconde que tous ces hommes de l'Asie orientale : Indiens, Chinois et Cochinchinois, Siamois, Cambodgiens, Japonais, dont les monuments longtemps ignorés sollicitent aujourd'hui notre étude et nous apportent tardivement la révélation d'un art si saisissant et si étrange. Chez eux aussi, la sculpture décorative, en pierre, en marbre, en bronze, prodigue ses inventions sur les édifices. Divinités monstrueuses, héros fantastiques, animaux formidables, créations extraordinaires d'une imagination en délire, décorent les tombeaux, les palais, les pagodes et les temples. Que d'études, là aussi, à pour-

suivre! que de découvertes à compléter! Mais ce serait dépasser les
bornes de cette introduction que d'insister ici sur cet art si intéres-
sant quoique si loin de nous, de nos traditions et de nos goûts;
hâtons-nous d'arriver à l'art classique, à la sculpture grecque.

Ici, le champ est immense. La Grèce fut la terre bénie de la
sculpture, et non seulement la Grèce, mais encore tous les pays où
l'hellénisme étendit son heureuse et féconde influence, comme l'Asie-
Mineure et l'Italie méridionale.

La sculpture sous toutes ses formes, ornements, figures, hauts et
bas-reliefs, ronde-bosse, embellit de bonne heure les monuments de
la Grèce antique : les deux lions affrontés de la porte de Mycènes
sont probablement les plus vieux morceaux de sculpture hellénique
qui nous soient parvenus, et il est intéressant de constater qu'ils
rentrent déjà franchement dans le domaine de l'art décoratif. La
décoration sculpturale apparut ainsi dès les premiers essais de l'art
grec, et, depuis, ne cessa jamais de se mêler aux combinaisons de
l'architecture : l'abondance et la qualité des incomparables matériaux
du pays, le système des constructions helléniques ne rendaient-ils
pas naturelle, inévitable, la continuelle intervention du sculpteur?
Les chapiteaux de colonnes, les frontons, les frises, les métopes,
n'appelaient-ils pas forcément le bas-relief ou la ronde-bosse? Le
fronton n'est-il pas un cadre tout préparé pour la sculpture? Les
angles des tympans ne réclament-ils pas les acrotères? Aussi voyons
nous, aussitôt après la courte période du dorique primitif, la sculp-
ture s'installer comme d'elle-même sur toutes ces surfaces et à toutes
ces places où elle fait si bien, parce qu'elle se soumet avec autant de
bonne grâce que de succès aux exigences de l'architecture et aux
nécessités de l'harmonie.

Aux tympans et aux métopes, à la lumière du grand jour, les
sculptures sont presque toujours de très haut relief; les frises
intérieures, au contraire, destinées à rester dans l'ombre, ont
généralement peu de saillie. C'est ainsi, on le sait, qu'était conçue
la décoration du Parthénon; c'est d'après ces règles si simples et
si logiques, que la sculpture de Phidias se mariait à l'architecture
d'Ictinus.

Je viens de citer le Parthénon; mais de combien de monuments
serait-il nécessaire encore d'étudier la décoration, pour donner une
idée vraie de ce que fut en Grèce l'alliance heureuse du sculpteur
et de l'architecte! Il est impossible ici de donner même un aperçu
sommaire de ce que fut dans l'Hellénie et ses dépendances la sculp-
ture décorative; il nous est interdit de décrire, même rapidement,
les diverses périodes et les transformations d'un art si fertile. Mais

au moins faut-il expressément rappeler que les Grecs ont laissé, pour la décoration scupturale plus encore que pour toute autre branche de la statuaire, des modèles et des principes, des types et des règles dont tous les peuples de culture gréco-latine relèvent encore aujourd'hui. De qui donc nous viennent, sinon des Grecs, tant de motifs ornementaux indéfiniment reproduits et copiés depuis : les oves, les tresses, les palmettes, les rais-de-chœur et les perles, avec les grecques, les feuilles d'eau, les volutes du chapiteau dorique et les feuilles d'acanthe du corinthien? A qui encore avons-nous emprunté le type si heureux de la statue-colonne, de la cariatide, sinon au peuple initiateur qui nous a laissé les Télamons colossaux d'Agrigente et les divines Canéphores du Pandrosion?

Avec abondance et discrétion à la fois, la sculpture n'a cessé ainsi de venir chez les Grecs à l'appui de l'architecture et de se montrer sous toutes les formes partout où l'architecte lui ménageait, aux chapiteaux comme aux frontons, dans le cadre étroit des métopes ou sur les longues bandes des entablements, des emplacements naturels et des cadres propices. Sauf pour la cariatide et le chapiteau, en effet, n'est-il pas à remarquer que la décoration sculpturale des Grecs se présente toujours comme « encadrée » dans l'architecture? Elle ne détonne jamais, jamais elle n'empiète; mais elle a le caractère d'un « ornement » : elle peut être absente et, de fait, l'a quelquefois été, comme dans les sévères monuments du dorique ancien. « Essayez, au contraire, comme dit très bien Eugène Véron, de l'arracher du monument égyptien : le monument s'écroulera. »

L'art romain, dérivé de l'art grec, n'a pas manqué de faire appel au sculpteur pour la décoration des monuments; mais rarement il a réalisé, moins soucieux que son modèle des nécessités de l'harmonie, la parfaite union de la statuaire et de l'architecture. Les ordres grecs, avec leurs chapiteaux élégants et leurs ornements traditionnels, ont été d'assez bonne heure importés en Italie; pour ajouter au corinthien quelque chose de plus somptueux et de plus fleuri, les Romains ont même inventé le « composite »; ils ont abondamment, eux aussi, répandu les bas-reliefs sur les surfaces libres de l'architecture; leurs édifices publics et privés, leurs monuments civils et religieux, leurs temples, leurs basiliques, leurs thermes, leurs villas, leurs colonnes triomphales, leurs tombeaux étaient couverts d'ornements sculptés et de bas-reliefs : le goût fastueux des maîtres de l'empire se plaisait à cette profusion décorative; mais la fusion complète des deux arts, l'accord entre la construction et l'ornement sont bien rares. Trop souvent, chez les Romains, la décoration se présente comme une applique, et l'on dirait presque un placage; trop souvent il n'y a plus

rien là qui ressemble à l'admirable unité du monument égyptien ni
à la belle harmonie de l'art grec.

Il y a pourtant une exception; il est un type de monument dans
lequel l'art romain unit et combine dans un harmonieux ensemble
l'art de l'architecte et celui du sculpteur : c'est l'arc de triomphe.
Quoi de plus orné, de la base à l'entablement, que l'arc de Constantin,
par exemple, avec ses chapiteaux, ses médaillons, ses frises, ses
bas-reliefs, ses renommées volantes au tympan des arcs, ses grandes
statues en ronde-bosse au-dessus des colonnes? Et quoi de plus un,
pourtant, quoi de plus homogène, que ce monument aux lignes si
fermes, aux proportions si justes?

Telle est la multiplicité et la variété des œuvres de décoration
scupturale laissées par les Romains sur tout le territoire d'un empire
qui allait de la Tamise au Nil et de Cadix à Balbeck, qu'il est impos-
sible d'en essayer ici une classification sérieuse : il y faudrait une
place dont nous ne disposons pas. Disons pourtant que la diversité
en est presque infinie; que le mérite artistique en est assez inégal et
va de l'excellent au médiocre; que l'intérêt historique en est toujours
extrêmement précieux. La religion et l'histoire fournissent, en effet,
la plupart des sujets de bas-reliefs; les empereurs romains ont voulu
éterniser sur le marbre, le bronze ou la pierre, les hauts faits de leur
principat : les guerres de Trajan revivent sur la colonne qui porte son
nom; les voyages et les expéditions d'Hadrien étaient représentés en
bas-reliefs dans les galeries intérieures d'un édifice grandiose, un
tombeau, qui est aujourd'hui le château Saint-Ange, et sur combien
d'autres monuments encore! Les cérémonies et les légendes religieuses
formaient une autre série de motifs : processions, théogonies, sacri-
fices; le culte de Mithra, l'histoire de Psyché, les mystères d'Éleusis,
toute la mythologie, depuis ses plus lointaines origines jusqu'aux der-
niers symboles alexandrins ou syriaques, s'étalait sur les parois des
édifices sacrés. L'histoire et la religion de Rome, interprétées le plus
souvent d'ailleurs par des artistes grecs, ornaient ainsi, concurrem-
ment avec les motifs de décoration pure, emblèmes, trophées, etc., les
monuments romains.

De la fin de l'empire romain aux commencements de l'art ogival,
des dernières basiliques aux premières cathédrales, durant une
longue et confuse période de six à sept siècles, l'art et le goût,
l'architecture, la sculpture, la décoration, désormais sans guide sûr
et universellement accepté, subirent toutes sortes d'influences diver-
ses et cherchèrent leur voie, oscillant entre les souvenirs inoubliables
de l'art gréco-romain et les aspirations, les recherches, les essais
d'un art en formation. S'inspirant des monuments antiques en les

transformant, les artistes originaires de ce qui avait été l'empire
d'Occident trouvèrent un type original et nouveau, l'architecture
romane; les artistes issus de ce qui était encore l'empire d'Orient
donnèrent naissance à l'art byzantin.

Ce que le byzantin et le roman eurent de différent ou de commun,
ce qu'ils conservèrent ou perdirent l'un et l'autre des traditions
antiques, nous ne saurions, même sommairement, l'indiquer ici. Nous
remarquerons seulement qu'avec tous les deux on vit se transformer
profondément le système et les procédés de la décoration sculpturale.
Les chrétiens d'Orient, dit Viollet-le-Duc, évasèrent le chapiteau,
élargirent son tailloir et « ne couvrirent ses faces nues que de fines
sculptures peu saillantes qui ne pouvaient en altérer la solidité ».
La sculpture s'efface donc et ressemble à de la gravure; elle fait
appel aux ressources du coloris ou, tout simplement, sur les surfaces
plates, cède la place à la mosaïque.

Chez les hommes de l'Occident la sculpture tient également assez
peu de place d'abord dans la décoration des monuments. Les chapi-
teaux cependant continuent à se parer des ornements traditionnels;
mais les anciens types s'altèrent, les volutes et les feuillages s'enflent
ou s'amaigrissent, la main de l'ouvrier s'alourdit. Ce n'est qu'à partir
du jour où, après les terreurs de l'an mil, le style roman est défini-
tivement constitué, que la sculpture décorative, déployant de nouveau
toutes ses ressources et retrouvant toutes les habiletés d'exécution,
redevient l'auxiliaire fidèle et inséparable de l'architecture. Aux
chapiteaux des colonnes, elle s'épanouit et s'égaie en toutes sortes
d'ornements géométriques ou de végétations fantastiques, aussi
variés d'invention que le chapiteau lui-même est varié dans sa forme.
Aux pilastres, aux arcades, elle adosse des statues ou modèle des
ornements de haut relief; dans les tympans, elle encadre de grandes
compositions symboliques et dessine des frises charmantes; aux
archivoltes elle met des moulures, des arabesques, des zigzags, des
rinceaux, des feuillages, et les portails des églises romanes font déjà
prévoir, par l'abondance de leur ornementation, la richesse et la
fantaisie des portails gothiques.

Le gothique! ce seul mot n'évoque-t-il pas dans l'esprit l'idée
d'une décoration prodigue, surabondante, merveilleuse, d'une profu-
sion d'ornements et de sculptures, d'un art où le statuaire est le
collaborateur assidu et fidèle, toujours docile et toujours présent, de
l'architecte écouté, accepté, obéi comme le vrai « maître de l'œuvre » ?
Il y a vraiment des édifices gothiques où tous les membres de
l'architecture et tous les éléments de la construction se sont tournés
en sculptures : portails, chapiteaux, rosaces, ogives et meneaux des

fenêtres, choux et dentelures des clochers, contreforts, stalles des chœurs, jubés, chaires, autels, tombeaux, dalles tumulaires, tout y devient pour l'architecte occasion d'appeler le statuaire à son aide; et telle est chez l'un et chez l'autre la volonté de tout subordonner à l'harmonie, à la beauté, à la perfection de l'œuvre commune, que toutes les parties de la décoration sont intimement liées à l'architecture, « aussi bien par la pensée générale, comme le dit si justement Eugène Véron, que par l'exécution dans le détail. » De là l'admirable unité de ces constructions si touffues et la prédominance de l'effet d'ensemble dans ces édifices où le détail fourmille, où les statues se comptent par milliers. On voit qu'il y eut là d'innombrables ouvriers, mais on sent qu'il n'y eut qu'une inspiration, qu'une volonté, qu'une âme. Ce sont littéralement des foules qui ont maçonné, fouillé, sculpté, mis en place toutes ces pierres, mais des foules disciplinées, pieusement soumises à la voix du maître, c'est-à-dire ici de l'architecte, à peu près comme les moines à l'abbé. L'abnégation de l'ouvrier contribue ainsi, ce fut sa récompense, à la sublimité de l'ouvrage.

La statuaire décorative au moyen âge est profondément originale et se distingue par des caractères tout à fait tranchés de l'art antérieur, ou du moins de l'art antique, qu'elle ignore. Aux XIIe et XIIIe siècles, toute sculpture, d'abord, est décorative, c'est-à-dire conçue et exécutée en vue d'un effet d'ensemble; les anonymes « tailleurs d'images » qui couvrent les monuments de sculptures s'oublient pour ne penser qu'à l'œuvre collective à laquelle ils ont reçu mission de consacrer leurs soins. Conformément aux prescriptions scrupuleusement suivies de l'architecte, ils concentrent sur certains points choisis les ornements ou les figures : les voussures deviennent comme une dentelle de pierre; les niches aux baldaquins délicatement fouillés abritent des statues; les chapiteaux reproduisent la flore variée du pays; les parties tranquilles font valoir les parties sculptées et chacune des parties travaillées l'est en vue de tout le reste; les dispositions sculpturales contribuent à préciser les lignes architectoniques. La statuaire ornementale est pourtant toujours traitée, au moyen âge, en ronde-bosse; mais, par une sorte de compensation, elle reste toujours aussi abritée par des motifs architecturaux, baldaquins, galeries, niches ou portails : ainsi l'exigent à la fois le climat et la prépondérance incontestée de l'architecte sur tous ses collaborateurs en ces temps ingénus. Ce que représente cette sculpture, dans la diversité charmante de ses inventions naïves, c'est la religion et la vie, c'est la réalité et en même temps le rêve et la pensée du temps; elle va ainsi du sublime à la caricature; elle est le lyrisme, étonnamment libre, exalté, quelquefois débridé, de ce moyen âge dont l'architecture est, selon le mot de Victor Hugo, la véritable épopée.

Telle est la profusion des œuvres de la statuaire dans l'art ogival, que tout édifice devient comme un musée de sculpture, et telle est la profusion des édifices gothiques répandus sur le sol de l'Europe, que le seul dénombrement en serait immense. Du gothique robuste et relativement simple de Notre-Dame de Paris au gothique flamboyant du Palais de Justice à Rouen, pour ne parler que de la France, que de monuments civils ou religieux! quelle variété! quelle fécondité! et toujours quel admirable sentiment de l'harmonie! quelle merveilleuse entente de la subordination des parties! quel délicat accord de la décoration et de la structure!

Ce serait ici le moment, si nous en avions la place, de parler de la sculpture sur bois, partout si florissante au moyen âge, et de tous ces chefs-d'œuvre de nos « hûchiers », coffres, rétables, jubés, stalles de chœur, etc., qui faisaient, à l'intérieur, l'ornement et la gloire des châteaux, des palais et des cathédrales. Mais ce serait sortir des bornes de cette préface et redire ce qu'a si bien dit M. de Lostalot dans son élégante introduction aux *Arts du Bois*. Pour tout ce qui regarde la sculpture sur bois à ses diverses périodes, nous renvoyons le lecteur à ce travail et au précieux album dont il forme l'Introduction.

Quand l'art ogival, en son plein et surabondant épanouissement, fut presque sans transition supplanté par l'art de la Renaissance; quand l'étude et l'admiration de l'antiquité, détournant tout à coup au XVe siècle artistes et public des voies originales suivies par les artistes de l'Occident, ramenèrent l'architecture et la sculpture à l'imitation de l'art grec et romain, on vit renaître les « ordres » avec les chapiteaux à volutes ou à feuilles d'acanthe; on vit les frises se couvrir de rinceaux et d'ornements de tout genre, les pilastres porter des figures ou des arabesques, les bas-reliefs s'appliquer aux parois libres des édifices, le bronze des portes monumentales se mouler en merveilleux reliefs, le ciseau des tailleurs de marbres fouiller les piliers et les colonnes, les cheminées, les portes, les consoles, les vases d'amortissement, les margelles de puits, les balustres, etc.; la sculpture décorative fleurit, s'épanouit, se répand en fantaisies réglées par un goût affiné à l'école des anciens.

Pour avoir vu et admiré quelques bas-reliefs antiques, Nicolas et Jean de Pise, puis André de Pise ouvrirent la route où marchèrent après eux les Lucca della Robbia, les Ghiberti, les Donatello, les Brunelleschi, les Sansovino, les Bandinelli, les Benvenuto Cellini, les Bernin et tant d'autres que nous ne pouvons même pas nommer ici.

D'Italie, l'admiration de l'antique et l'esprit de la Renaissance passent en France, en Allemagne, en Espagne, où le génie propre de chaque pays se les approprie en les modifiant. Citons seulement, presque au hasard, les décorations merveilleuses, les sculptures, les meubles monumentaux, les boiseries de tels ou tels monuments français, comme les châteaux de Gaillon, de Chenonceaux, de Chambord, de Blois, d'Anet, ou les palais des Tuileries et du Louvre. Rappelons les chefs-d'œuvre d'art décoratif du grand siècle qui porte le nom de Louis XIV, les merveilles de Versailles, qu'on admire encore, ou celles de Marly, qui ne sont plus qu'un souvenir. Nommons aussi en passant quelques-uns de nos grands artistes des xvie et xviie siècles : Michel Colomb, Jean Goujon, Germain Pilon, Girardon, Puget, Coysevox, Coustou et ce Lebrun qui n'était pas sculpteur, mais dont les dessins ont inspiré toute une école de sculpture ornementale dont le goût noble et fécond se retrouve en tant d'œuvres de son temps.

Aussi, à partir de Louis XIV et pour un siècle et demi, n'est-ce plus en Italie surtout, mais en France, que le monde civilisé vint chercher des modèles; c'est Versailles d'abord que l'on copia; plus tard, ce fut le style Louis XV, puis le style Louis XVI que l'on imita partout. Quels grands et charmants décorateurs, en effet, que tous ces artistes du bois, du bronze ou de la pierre dont les hôtels et les appartements du xviiie siècle abritèrent les charmantes créations, d'une tournure si imprévue et si gracieuse au temps du Régent, de la Pompadour ou de la Dubarry, d'un goût si élégant, si fin, si pur à l'époque de Marie-Antoinette! Alors furent sculptées, ciselées ou fondues ces délicates merveilles dont ce qui subsiste encore n'a plus de prix et dont nos décorateurs modernes, désespérant d'inventer, reproduisent indéfiniment les types. On en verra plus loin des reproductions charmantes, et l'on comprendra mieux par ces images que par les analyses ou les descriptions les plus consciencieuses le charme exquis de ces décorations si ingénieuses et si variées, exécutées, en toute matière, d'une main si précise et si souple.

Le style Empire, qui crut corriger et ennoblir le Louis XVI, ne fit souvent que le guinder, le raidir et lui enlever, sous prétexte de noblesse et de retour à l'antique, sa grâce et sa fantaisie. Fontaine et Percier furent les Lebrun de cet art prétentieux et froid : ils crurent créer un style et ne trouvèrent qu'une manière. Il y a pourtant quelquefois un certain charme austère dans les motifs d'ornementation dessinés par leur crayon rigide; les hauts prix atteints par plus d'une œuvre décorative et par plus d'un meuble de leur école et de leur temps ne sont pas le pur effet de l'engouement et de la mode.

Depuis, le goût s'est fait éclectique. La sculpture décorative, comme l'architecture, a imité, très heureusement parfois, la Renaissance italienne ou française, le style Louis XIV, le Louis XV, le Louis XVI, parfois même l'Empire. Aujourd'hui même nos édifices se couvrent volontiers de sculptures; les municipalités et l'État offrent à la sculpture décorative mille occasions de se déployer. Plus d'une œuvre exquise a ainsi vu le jour. La *Flore*, de Carpeaux, au Pavillon de Flore; le *Génie des Arts*, de Mercié, au fronton du Louvre; la *Jeunesse*, de Chapu, sur le monument de Regnault; le *Mirabeau et Dreux-Brézé*, de Dalou, à la Chambre des députés, sont la parure et l'honneur des monuments qui les renferment.

Mais le vrai sens décoratif, il faut bien le dire, n'est pas commun chez nos artistes. La sculpture monumentale fait volontiers profession d'ignorer l'architecture et ses convenances. Sous prétexte d'indépendance et de dignité, le sculpteur refuse trop facilement de se préoccuper du style et de l'harmonie des monuments qu'il décore. L'architecte n'est généralement admis à choisir ni les sujets à traiter, ni les artistes qui les traiteront : c'est affaire administrative. Il n'exerce aucun contrôle sérieux sur l'acceptation des projets; presque toujours, il dédaigne de s'en occuper, trop assuré d'avance que ses observations seraient inutiles et mal acceptées. Il laisse faire, et les sculpteurs désignés par la division des Beaux-Arts se mettent à décorer à qui mieux mieux nos édifices publics, sans s'entendre avec l'architecte, sans lui parler, sans le voir, sans s'entendre, se parler et se voir entre eux. C'est ainsi qu'on arrive à d'étranges cacophonies.

Mais n'insistons pas. Rappelons seulement, pour terminer, cette grande loi de l'art décoratif et cette vérité de sens commun : que tout décor nuit à l'ensemble et se nuit à lui-même, qui méconnaît la règle des subordinations nécessaires et refuse de s'accommoder aux exigences supérieures de l'unité et de l'harmonie. Approprier son œuvre aux conditions d'un ensemble qui la domine et la soutient, n'est pas déchoir et capituler : c'est grandir. Dans l'art, comme à la guerre, une certaine discipline est la condition et le gage des grandes victoires.

Louis BAUZON.

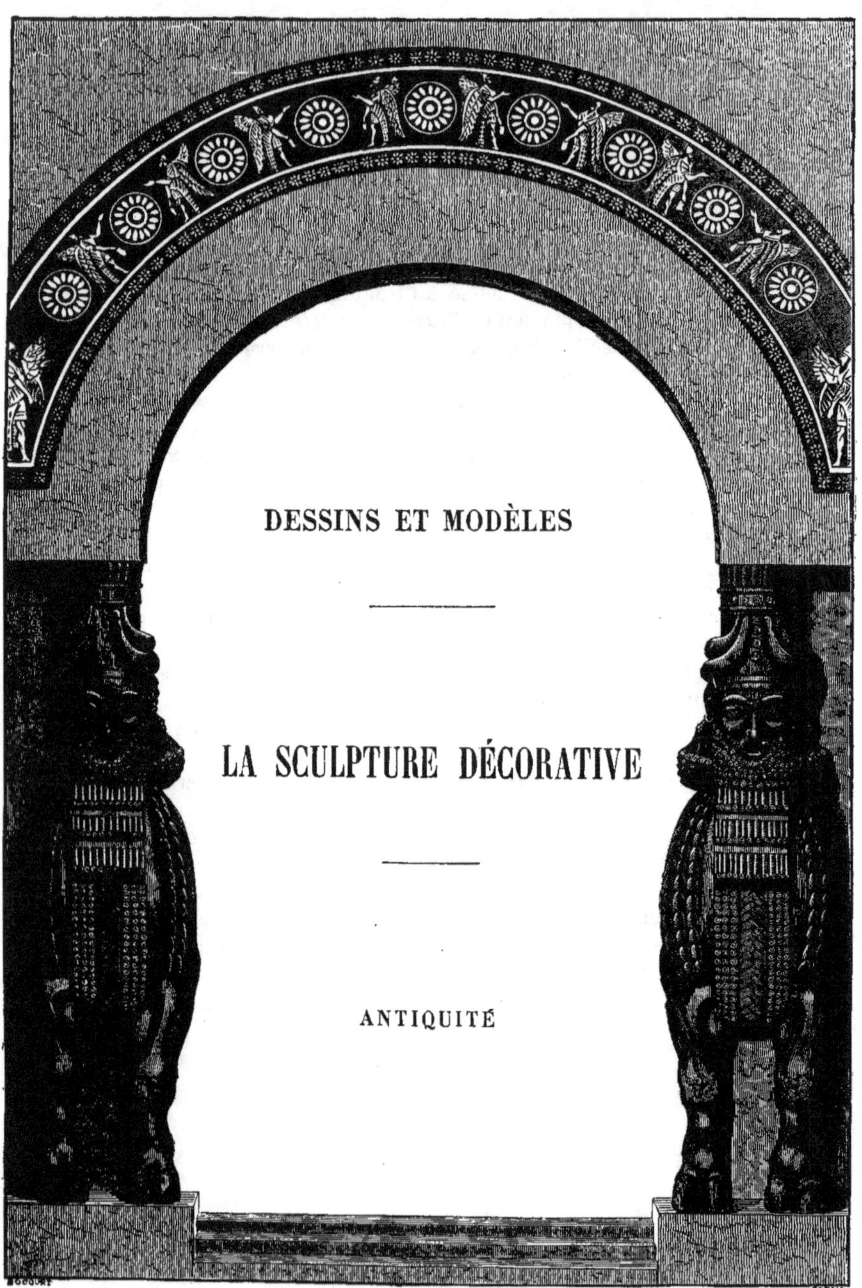

PORTE MONUMENTALE DE LA VILLE DE HISIR-SARGON (Khorsabad) EN ASSYRIE.

ENTRÉE DU GRAND TEMPLE D'IBSAMBOUL.

BAS-RELIEF DE LA TOMBE DE TI, ANCIEN EMPIRE (ÉGYPTE).

(Moulage du Musée du Louvre.)

GRAND SPHINX DE L'ÉPOQUE DES PASTEURS (ÉGYPTE).

BAS-RELIEF DE LA TOMBE DE TI, ANCIEN EMPIRE (ÉGYPTE).

(Moulage du Musée du Louvre.)

LION ÉGYPTIEN.

LIONNE BLESSÉE.

(Bas-relief du Musée Britannique.)

ENTABLEMENT CORINTHIEN.

VASE A PARFUMS EN TERRE CUITE TROUVÉ A KERTCH (PANTICAPÉE).

(Musée de l'Ermitage, à Saint-Pétersbourg.)

VASE A PARFUMS EN TERRE-CUITE TROUVE A KERTCH (PANTICAPÉE).

(Musée de l'Ermitage, à Saint-Pétersbourg.)

CHAPITEAU DE PILASTRE.

(Temple de Didymes.)

CHAPITEAU DE PILASTRE.

(Temple de Didymes.)

TRÔNE D'APOLLON AMYCLÉEN.

LA VICTOIRE AUX SANDALES.

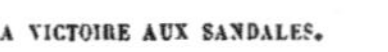

LA VICTOIRE AU TAUREAU.

(Fragments de la balustrade du Temple de la Victoire Aptère, à Athènes.)

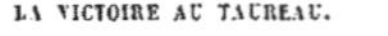

EX-VOTO A LA MÈRE DES DIEUX.

(Bas-relief du Musée de Berlin, trouvé à Athènes.)

BACCHUS ET ARIADNE.

(Collection de M. de Nolivos.)

LIT EN MARBRE DU TOMBEAU DE PYDNA, EN MACÉDOINE.

SATYRE ET CHÈVRE.

(D'après une pierre gravée antique.)

AMPHITRITE, PAR GLYCON.

(Sardonyx du Cabinet des médailles.)

BASE DODÉCAGONE.

(Temple de Didymes.)

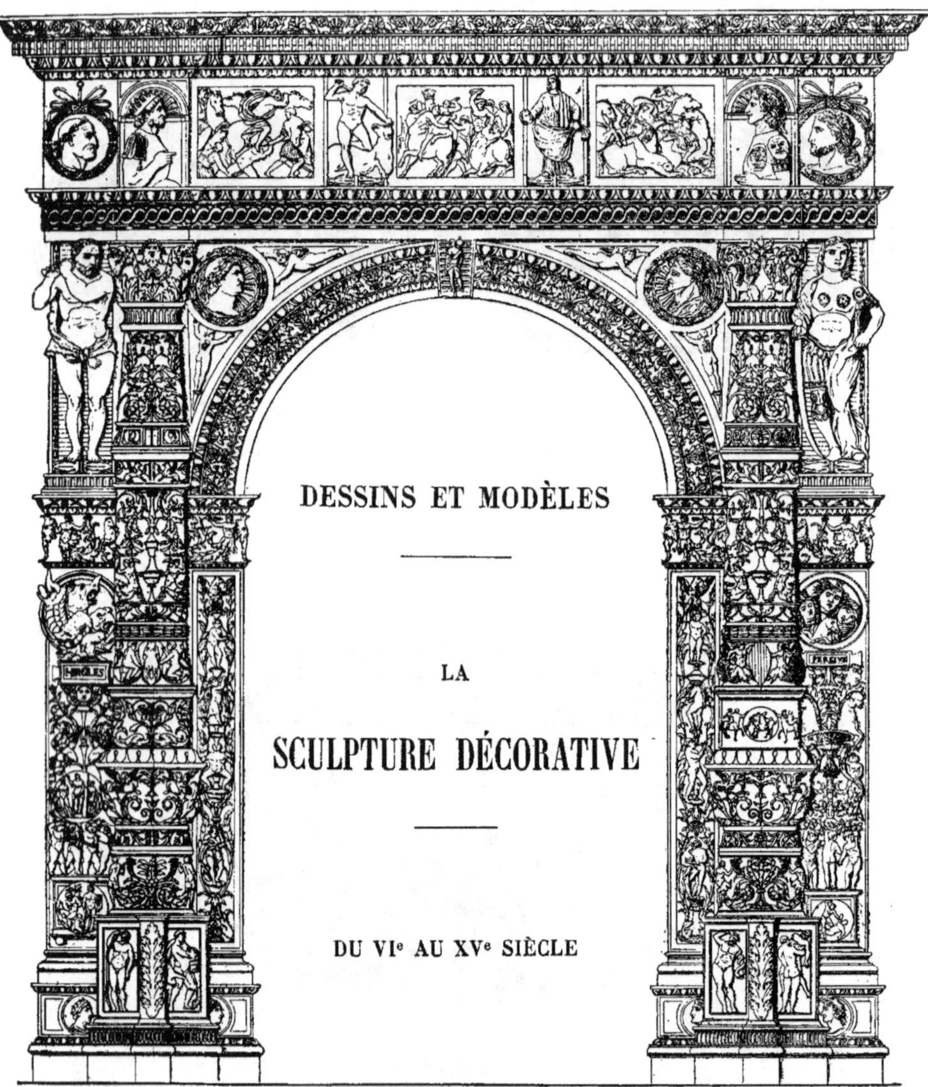

ENCADREMENT D'APRÈS LA PORTE DU PALAIS STANGA, A CRÉMONE.

(Musée du Louvre.)

DIPTYQUE DE NOVARE, IVOIRE DU VI° SIÈCLE.

(Trésor de la cathédrale de Novare.)

CATHÉDRALE DE SAINT-DIMITRI, A VLADIMIR (RUSSIE).

(XIIe siècle.)

PLAQUE COMMÉMORATIVE DE LA FONDATION DE L'ÉGLISE SAINTE-CATHERINE EN MÉMOIRE DE LA BATAILLE DE BOUVINES.

LE JUGEMENT DERNIER.

(Bas-relief de la façade du Dôme d'Orvieto. — Fin du XIIIᵉ siècle.)

TOMBEAU DE JEAN SANS-PEUR, DUC DE BOURGOGNE, ET DE MARGUERITE DE BAVIÈRE.

DALLE TUMULAIRE DE JEHAN D'HESTOMESNIL ET DE PH. LE-OUDEUR, DE LOGNY, SON NEVEU (1361).

PIERRE TUMULAIRE DE JEHAN, CHANOINE DE NOYON († 1350).

FRAGMENT DE RÉTABLE DE L'AUTEL DU « CORPUS DOMINI ».

(Église San-Lorenzo de Vicence.)

PORTES DE BRONZE DANS L'ÉGLISE DE SAINT-PIERRE-AUX-LIENS, A ROME.

ENTABLEMENT DE LA CHAPELLE DES PORTINARI, A MILAN.

BAS-RELIEF EN MARBRE, TRAVAIL ITALIEN DU XVe SIÈCLE.

(Appartenant à M. Châtel.)

MADONE DE TERRE CUITE PEINTE ET DORÉE, BAS-RELIEF ITALIEN DU XVᵉ SIÈCLE.

(Musée du Louvre.)

ANIMAUX FANTASTIQUES EN PIERRE SCULPTÉE.

(Château de Pierrefonds.)

FIGURES D'ENFANTS, PAR DONATELLO.

(Bronzes de la collection de M. Eugène Piot.)

MONTANT GAUCHE DE LA PORTE DU PALAIS STANGA, A CRÉMONE.

(Musée du Louvre.)

MONTANT DROIT DE LA PORTE DU PALAIS STANGA, A CRÉMONE.

(Musée du Louvre.)

TYMPAN GAUCHE ET STATUE D'HERCULE.

TYMPAN DROIT ET STATUE DE PERSÉE.

DÉTAILS DE LA PORTE DU PALAIS STANGA, A CRÉMONE.

(Musée du Louvre.)

FIGURES D'ANGES, BAS-RELIEFS EN TERRE CUITE DU VERROCCHIO. (Collection de M. Thiers, au Musée du Louvre.)

FIGURE DE LA VIERGE.

(Clôture du Chœur de la Cathédrale d'Albi.)

CLÔTURE DU CHŒUR DE LA CATHÉDRALE D'ALBI.

LE PUITS DE MOÏSE, PAR CLAUX SLUTER, XVᵉ SIÈCLE.

(Chartreuse de Dijon.)

LE PUITS DE MOÏSE, PAR CLAUX SLUTER, XVᵉ SIÈCLE.

(Chartreuse de Dijon.)

PILIER DE LA FAÇADE DU DÔME D'ORVIETO.

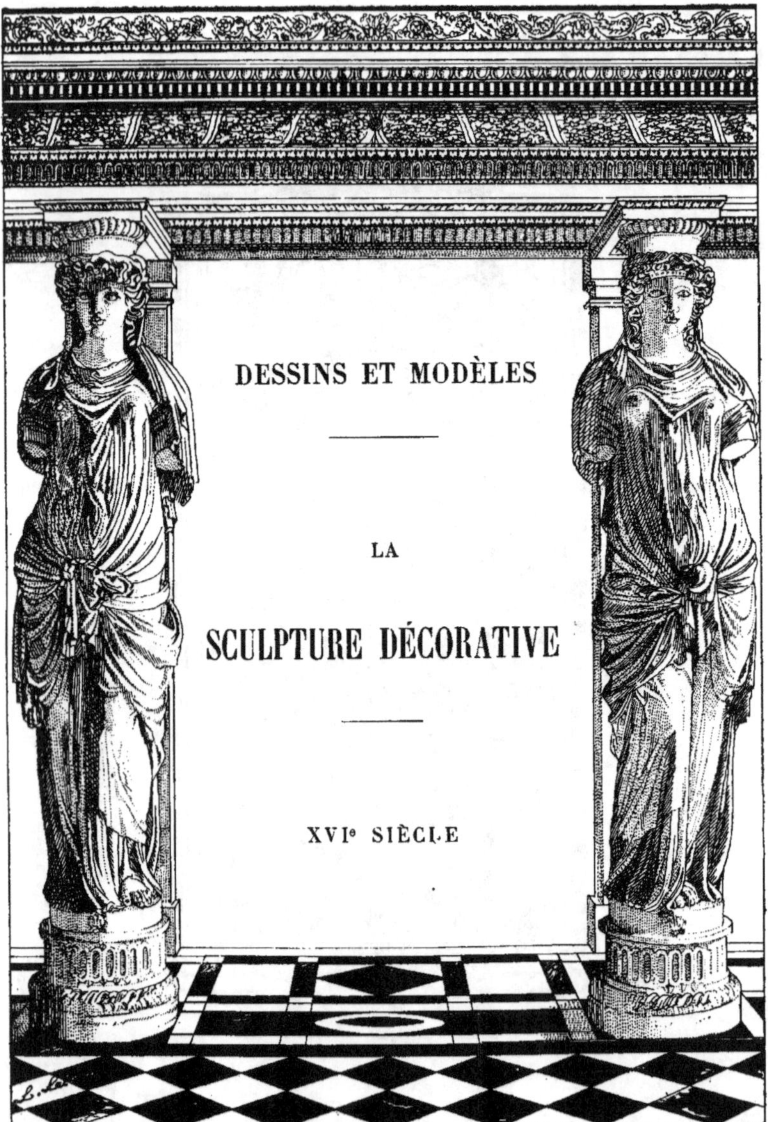

ENCADREMENT D'APRÈS LA TRIBUNE DE LA SALLE DES CARIATIDES, AU LOUVRE.

LA SCULPTURE DÉCORATIVE.　　　　　8

LA JUSTICE.

(Cariatide du Mausolée de Claude de Lorraine, à la Mairie de Joinville.)

LA PEINTURE ET LA SCULPTURE. (Embrasure de l'une des portes du grand salon du château de Saint-Roch.)

TRITON ET NÉRÉIDE, BAS-RELIEF DE LA FONTAINE DES INNOCENTS.

(Sculpture de Jean Goujon, au Musée du Louvre.)

NYMPHES DE LA FONTAINE DES INNOCENTS, PAR JEAN GOUJON.

BAS-RELIEF EN MARBRE DE 1508.

(Collection Spitzer.)

PILASTRES DU TOMBEAU DE GASTON DE FOIX.

(Musée de Turin.

TROPHÉES D'ARMES DU TOMBEAU DE GASTON DE FOIX.

(Musée de Turin.)

TROPHÉES D'ARMES DU TOMBEAU DE GASTON DE FOIX.

(Musée de Turin.)

BAS-RELIEFS DU RÉTABLE DE SAINT-MERRI, PAR PIERRE BERTON DE SAINT-QUENTIN.

LA CÈNE, BAS-RELIEF DE FRANÇOIS GENTIL.

STATUE DE GUILLAUME DE LANGEY.

(Cathédrale du Mans.)

LA DIANE D'ANET, PAR JEAN GOUJON.

(Groupe en marbre du Musée du Louvre.)

AUTEL DE LA CHAPELLE D'ÉCOUEN, PAR JEAN BULLANT.

BAS-RELIEF, PAR JEAN GOUJON.

LE TOMBEAU DE L'AMIRAL CHABOT AUX CÉLESTINS.

FRISE DU TOMBEAU DE CHARLES D'ANJOU

TOMBEAU D'ARTUS GOUFFIER, GRAND-MAÎTRE DE FRANCE.

(Chapelle d'Oiron.)

TOMBEAU DE PHILIPPE DE MONTMORENCY, FEMME DE GUILLAUME GOUFFIER.

(Chapelle d'Oiron.)

PROJET D'ENSEMBLE DU TOMBEAU DE JULES II.

(D'après un dessin de Michel-Ange, conservé à la Galerie des Offices.)

LES TROIS GRACES DE GERMAIN PILON.

(Musée du Louvre.)

LA RENOMMÉE DE CADILLAC, PAR PIERRE BIARD.

(Musée du Louvre.)

CHIFFRE DE LA REINE CLAUDE.

(Château de Blois.)

CHIFFRE ET EMBLÈMES DE LA REINE CLAUDE.

(Château de Blois.)

GRANDE BALUSTRADE DU BATIMENT DE FRANÇOIS Ier.

(Château de Blois.)

CHIFFRE DU ROI FRANÇOIS Ier.

(Château de Blois.)

SALAMANDRE ROYALE.

(Château de Blois.)

EMBLÈMES DE LA REINE CLAUDE.

(Château de Blois.)

NÉRÉIDE, BAS-RELIEF DE LA FONTAINE DES INNOCENTS.

(Sculpture de Jean Goujon, au Musée du Louvre.)

OEIL-DE-BOEUF, PAR JEAN GOUJON.

(Cour du Louvre.)

FRAGMENT DE DÉCORATION RENAISSANCE.

LA CÈNE, SCULPTURE DE PIERRE BERTON POUR LE RÉTABLE DE SAINT-MERRI.

ENSEMBLE DU TOMBEAU DE JULIEN DE MÉDICIS.

(Chapelle Saint-Laurent, à Florence.)

ENSEMBLE DU TOMBEAU DE LAURENT DE MÉDICIS PAR MICHEL-ANGE.

Chapelle Saint-Laurent. — Florence.

PANNEAU DE PORTE DU CHATEAU D'ANET.

(Musée de l'École des Beaux-Arts.)

MÉDAILLON PROVENANT DU CHATEAU DE GAILLON.

(Musée de l'École des Beaux-Arts.)

ARC DE L'HOTEL TORPANE.

(Musée de l'École des Beaux-Arts.)

PORTE DE LA TOURELLE DE LA POISSONNIÈRE.

ARC DE L'HOTEL TORPANE.

(Musée de l'École des Beaux-Arts.)

TOMBEAU DES ENFANTS DE CHARLES VIII.

TOMBEAU DE THOMAS JAMES, A DOL.

SIÈGE DUCAL EN BOIS SCULPTÉ.

(Trésor de Saint-Marc, à Venise.)

PROJET DE TOMBEAU.

(Dessin de l'École italienne. — Musée du Louvre.)

TOMBEAU DE MICHEL-ANGE, A SANTA-CROCE.

MASQUE DE FAUNE, PAR MICHEL-ANGE.

(Musée national de Florence.)

ENCADREMENT, PAR RUBENS.

(D'après un dessin de l'Albertina, à Vienne.)

TYMPAN DE LA PORTE D'ENTRÉE DE L'HOTEL CARNAVALET, A PARIS.

(Sculpture de Germain Pilon ou de son école.)

BAS-RELIEF DE L'HOTEL CARNAVALET, A PARIS.

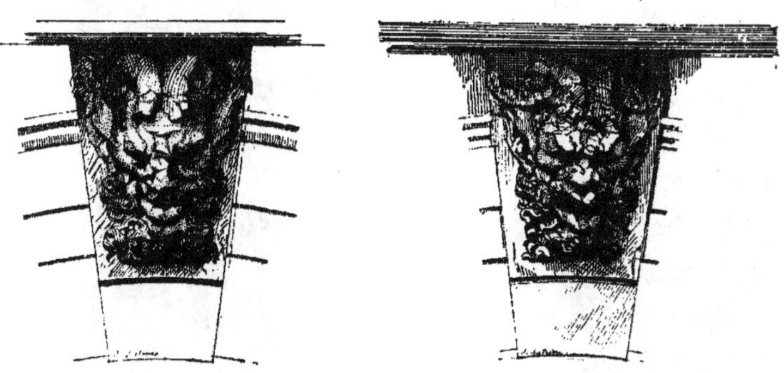

MASCARONS DE L'HOTEL CARNAVALET, A PARIS.

SCULPTURE DE L'HOTEL CARNAVALET, A PARIS.

FIGURE DE L'AIR A L'HOTEL CARNAVALET, A PARIS.

FIGURE DE CÉRÈS A L'HOTEL CARNAVALET, A PARIS.

VÉNUS ACCROUPIE, PAR COYSEVOX.

(Réplique de l'antique.)

BAS-RELIEF A GAUCHE DE LA PORTE D'ENTRÉE DE L'HOTEL CARNAVALET, A PARIS.

MARIE-ADÉLAÏDE DE SAVOIE, DUCHESSE DE BOURGOGNE, SOUS LA FIGURE DE DIANE, PAR COYSEVOX.

BAS-RELIEF A DROITE DE LA PORTE D'ENTRÉE DE L'HOTEL CARNAVALET, A PARIS.

CARIATIDE DE L'HOTEL DE VILLE DE TOULON, PAR PIERRE PUGET.

CARIATIDE DE L'HOTEL DE VILLE DE TOULON, PAR PIERRE PUGET.

SAINT SÉBASTIEN, PAR PIERRE PUGET.

SAINT SÉBASTIEN, IVOIRE D'ALONSO CANO.

(Collection de M. Thiers, au Louvre.)

ANTOINE COYSEVOX, PAR LUI-MÊME.

LA VIERGE ET L'ENFANT, PAR COYSEVOX.

(Église Saint-Nizier, à Lyon.)

PORTE EN BOIS DE L'ÉGLISE SAINT-LOUIS-EN-L'ILE.

(Sculpture décorative du XVIIe siècle.)

ANCIEN COUVENT DES DAMES DU CALVAIRE.

(Petit Luxembourg, XVIIe siècle.)

PROJET DE FONTAINE, PAR OPPENORT.

FONTAINE MÉDICIS AU JARDIN DU LUXEMBOURG, CONSTRUITE PAR SALOMON DE BROSSE.

(XVIIᵉ siècle.)

FONTAINE DE LA RUE CHILDEBERT, TRANSPORTÉE AU SQUARE MONGE, XVIIIe SIÈCLE.

(D'après les « Motifs historiques d'architecture » par César Daly.)

PORTE DE L'HOTEL DES MONNAIES, XVIII° SIÈCLE.

(D'après les « Motifs historiques d'architecture » par César Daly.)

BOISERIES PROVENANT D'UNE MAISON DE LA RUE DUMÉRIL, A PARIS.

(XVIIIe siècle.)

BOISERIES PROVENANT D'UNE MAISON DE LA RUE DUMÉRIL, A PARIS.

(Commencement du XVIIIᵉ siècle.)

GROUPE CENTRAL DE LA FONTAINE DE LA RUE DE GRENELLE, PAR BOUCHARDON.

(XVIIIᵉ siècle.)

LA TOILETTE DE VÉNUS.

(Bas-relief, par Clodion.)

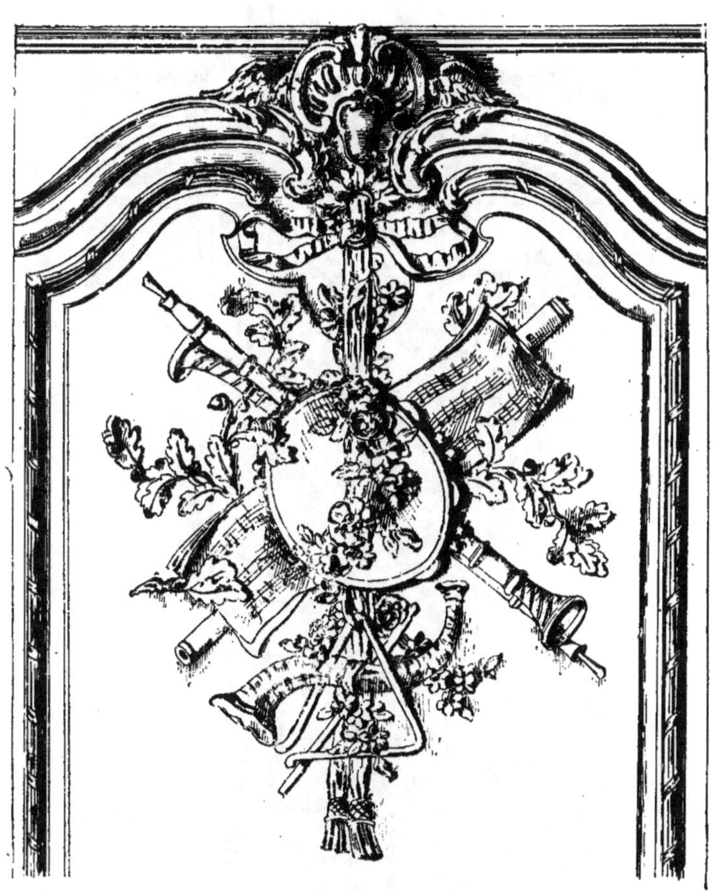

PANNEAU EN BOIS SCULPTÉ PROVENANT DE L'HOTEL DES STUARTS, XVIIIe SIÈCLE.

(Musée de l'hôtel Carnavalet.)

DÉCORATION DE L'UN DES SALONS DU MINISTÈRE DES TRAVAUX PUBLICS, PAR LEROUX.

(ANCIEN HOTEL ROQUELAURE. — XVIIIᵉ SIÈCLE.)

(D'après l'*Art architectural en France*, par A. Darcel et E. Royer.)

MONUMENT FUNÉRAIRE DU XVIIIᵉ SIÈCLE.

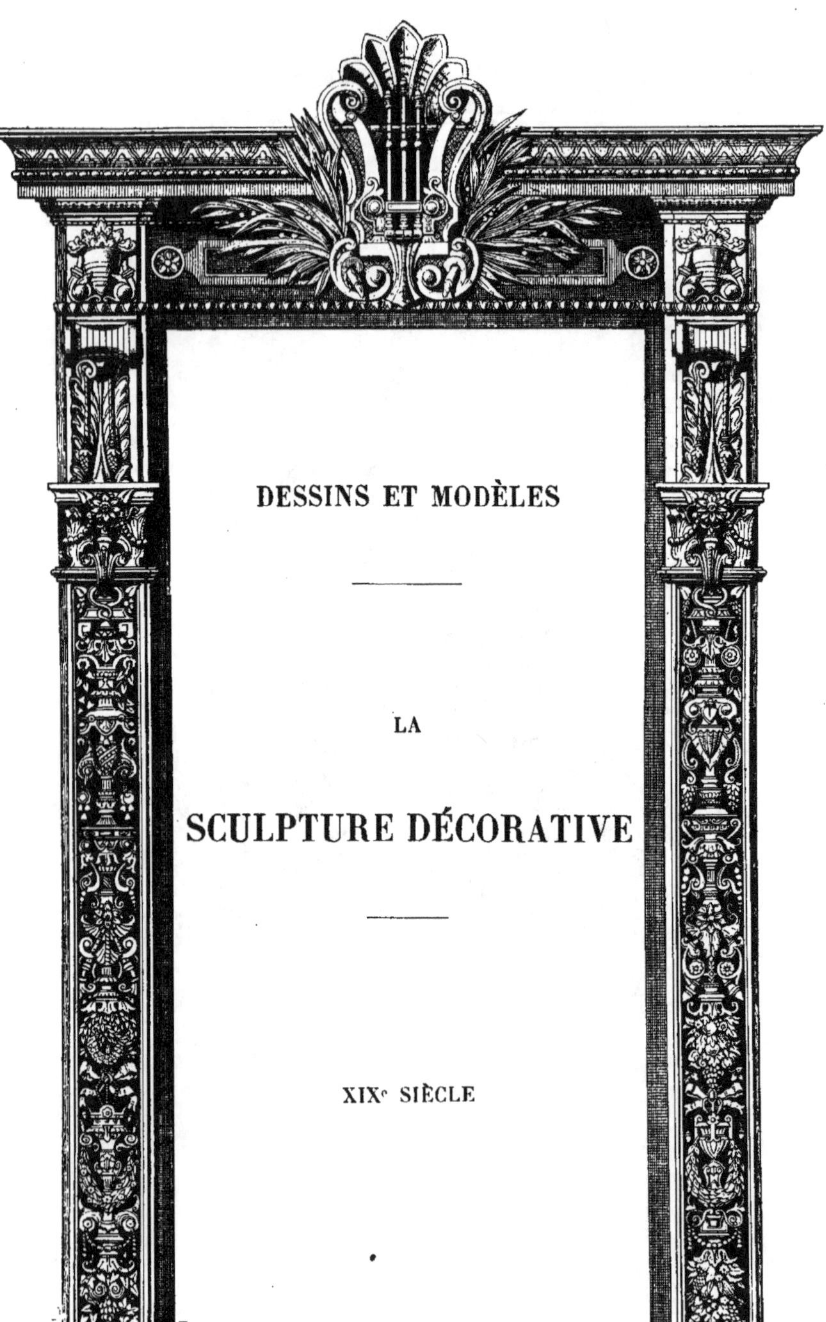

ENCADREMENT DE L'UNE DES PORTES DU GRAND FOYER, A L'OPÉRA.

ENSEMBLE DU TOMBEAU DE LA MORICIÈRE, PAR M. PAUL DUBOIS.

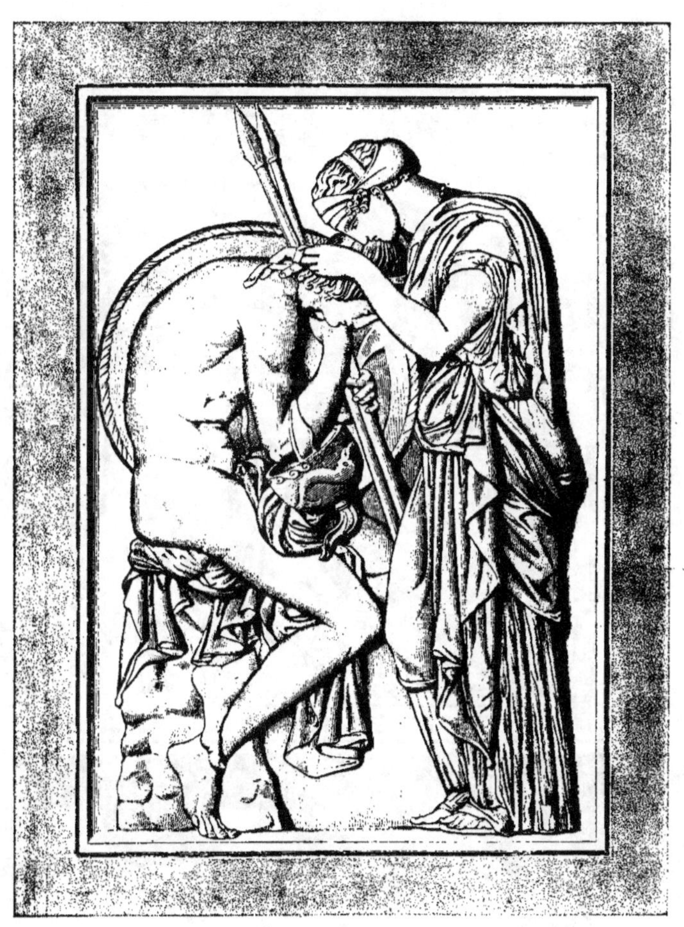

ETHRA PLEURANT SUR LA TÊTE DE PHALANTE, BAS-RELIEF EN CIRE, PAR GIRAUD.

(Musée de l'École des Beaux-Arts.)

REVERS DE LA FONTAINE MÉDICIS, AU JARDIN DU LUXEMBOURG, PAR VALOIS.

(Ancienne fontaine de la rue du Regard.)

GROUPE COURONNANT LE PAVILLON DE FLORE, AUX TUILERIES,
PAR CARPEAUX.

L'INNOCENCE IMPLORANT LA JUSTICE, PAR DAVID D'ANGERS.

(Œil-de-bœuf de la cour du Louvre.)

FRONTON DU MUSÉUM DE NANTES.

(Sculpture de M. G. Grootaers.)

HÉBÉ ET L'AIGLE.

(Bas-relief en marbre, par Hubac.)

LE BOEUF, PAR M. CAÏN.

(Dessin de l'artiste.)

THÉSÉE COMBATTANT LE CENTAURE BIÉNOR, GROUPE PAR BARYE.

(Musée du Puy.)

LIONNE, PAR BARYE.

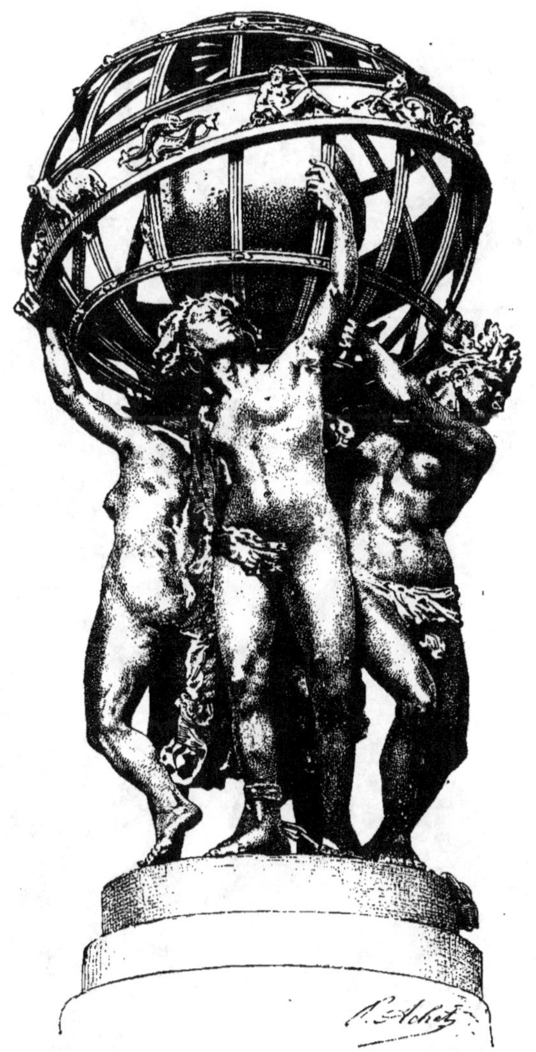

LES QUATRE PARTIES DU MONDE SOUTENANT LA SPHÈRE, PAR CARPEAUX.

(Fontaine de l'Observatoire.)

LE GROUPE DE LA DANSE, A L'OPÉRA, PAR CARPEAUX.

UGOLIN ET SES ENFANTS, PAR CARPEAUX.

HÉBÉ ENDORMIE, PAR M. CARRIER-BELLEUSE.

VASE EN MARBRE, PAR CHAPU.

(Hôtel N. de Rothschild, à Vienne. — Dessin de l'artiste.)

GROUPE EN BRONZE ET MARBRE, PAR CHAPU.

(Hôtel N. de Rothschild, à Vienne. — Dessin de l'artiste.)

LA MUSIQUE.

(Figure en plâtre, par Delaplanche.)

LA NATURE.

(Cariatide, par Chapu.)

LA TRADITION.

(Cariatide, par Chapu.)

L'IMMORTALITÉ, PAR M. LONGEPIED.

(Dessin de l'artiste.)

MASCARONS.

(Palais du Trocadéro.)

ÉCUSSON DE LA FRANCE SURMONTANT LA PORTE D'HONNEUR DU PALAIS DU CHAMP-DE-MARS EN 1878.

LA FORTUNE, PAR M. MOREAU-VAUTHIER.

LE DANSEUR NAPOLITAIN, PAR F. DURET.

MÉDAILLONS, PAR CHAPU.

MÉDAILLONS, PAR CHAPU.

FUT DE COLONNE. (Grand foyer de l'Opéra.)

CHAPITEAUX.

(Escalier d'honneur de l'Opéra.)

GÉNIE GARDANT LE SECRET DE LA TOMBE.

(Sculpture par M. de Saint-Marceaux.)

SÉMIRAMIS, SCULPTURE DE M. HÉBERT.

(Buste en bronze.)

MASCARON.
(Opéra).

BIBLIOTHÈQUE NATIONALE
RF
IMPRIMÉS

TABLE DES MATIÈRES

TABLE DES GRAVURES

BAS-RELIEFS

BOISERIES

CHAPITEAUX. — ENTABLEMENTS. — COLONNES
CARIATIDES. — MASCARONS

ENCADREMENTS

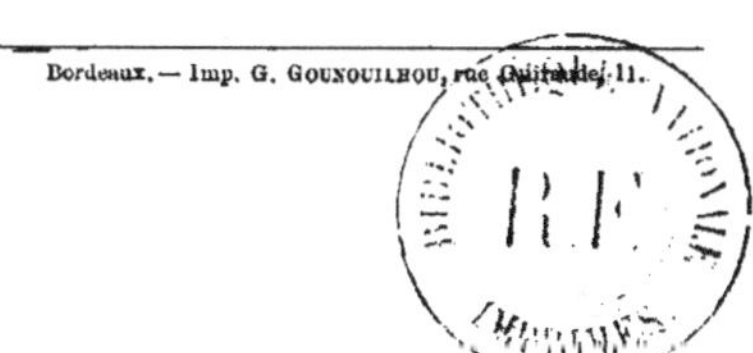

Bordeaux. — Imp. G. GOUNOUILHOU, rue Guiraude, 11.